The Perfect Date

CH

The Perfect Date

EVELYN LOZADA

WITH HOLLY LORINCZ

ST. MARTIN'S GRIFFIN

NEW YORK

THE PERFECT DATE. Copyright © 2019 by Evelyn Lozada. All rights reserved. Printed in the United States of America. For information, address St. Martin's Press, 175 Fifth Avenue, New York, N.Y. 10010.

www.stmartins.com

Designed by Omar Chapa

Frontispiece: *Cabeza* by Ángel Botello (Spanish-Puerto Rican painter, 1913–1986), c. 1940, oil on Masonite, 14¾ × 12⅞ inches, courtesy of Juan Botello

The Library of Congress Cataloging-in-Publication Data is available upon request.

ISBN 978-1-250-20488-2 (trade paperback)
ISBN 978-1-250-12500-2 (ebook)

Our books may be purchased in bulk for promotional, educational, or business use. Please contact your local bookseller or the Macmillan Corporate and Premium Sales Department at 1-800-221-7945, extension 5442, or by email at MacmillanSpecialMarkets@macmillan.com.

First Edition: June 2019

10 9 8 7 6 5 4 3 2

To my friends and family, who have offered support
and encouragement.

For the loves of my life, Shaniece and Leo,
I do it all for you.

Acknowledgments

I would like to acknowledge first and foremost, Sha and Leo, who are the blood flow to my heart and the motivating forces who give me the strength and courage to explore uncharted waters. I would also like to acknowledge my mom, who's shown me how positive change combats complexity. I love where we are. To my grandpa, I am so joyful we found you and for the memories we will make; my sister, I hope you know how much you mean to me; my nieces Mia and Nisa, my personal cheerleading squad, your bright futures await; and Iyanla Vanzant, thank you for being my accountability partner.

I am also grateful to those who gave a portion of their lives to complete this book: award-winning writer Holly L. Lorincz, thank you for cultivating my vision; my agent, Chip; and the many other people who worked to edit, typeset, and launch this story.

Last but not least, to the readers of this book . . . I hope you enjoy it! These pages are for you, a place I can share some of my hard-earned wisdom regarding strength and personal growth, especially as I have come to realize the power of choice, the risks and benefits of following the status quo, and not being afraid to break a cycle. My personal mandate for growth is unapologetic, calculated, and results-driven. I choose to accept or deny the life experiences that will be woven into the fabric of my being. So can you.

The Perfect Date

Chapter One

Angel Gomez hissed under her breath.

Claro. Of course. If she was going to get a paper cut, it would be from the page illustrating the male reproductive system. The twenty-three-year-old sucked at the thin line of blood on the web of her hand, squinting hard at the flayed *cojones* in her anatomy textbook.

As a nursing student, Angel knew the male anatomy—from the bulb to the external urinary meatus—but her ability to reel off the Latin names of penis parts seemed to scare the living, breathing version away.

Not that I want a man, she reminded herself, her inner voice stern. *Focus, girl.*

Dark spirals of hair popped free from her ponytail as she bent closer to her textbook. Concentration was elusive. She closed the window next to her with a shriek of metal on metal, shutting out the gray February breeze and the number 4 train running on the elevated tracks down Jerome Avenue. She tilted her head, listened.

What is that?

Breathing. It was gaspy, heavy breathing, coming from the depths of the worn corduroy couch behind her.

Angel twisted in her chair. "Jose," she said, too loudly, knocking pages of lecture notes off her makeshift desk on the radiator.

"Mama, I'm fine," the seven-year-old boy muttered. He turned up the live radio stream coming from the decrepit laptop and avoided her eyes.

"Go get your inhaler. Now."

"Just a minute. The Duke is about to pitch."

Faintly, she could hear Suzyn Waldman, longtime announcer for the Bronx Bolts, adding color to a local charity game. *"He's winding up and . . . another beauty, right over the plate . . . Ohh no, the batter's hit a hard foul right into the dugout."* The announcer clucked, but then, *"What's this? The Duke seems to want off the mound."*

"No!" Jose yelled at the computer, as if it could hear his complaint.

"His ankle may still be giving him problems."

"Jose! What'd I tell you?"

Jose's face shone with perspiration as he stomped past her, wheezing down the hall to his room. *That beautiful pouty face,* she thought. His bronze complexion, a shade darker than hers, was the perfect blend of her and his father. Jose's dad was long gone, however—the high school quarterback had disappeared when he found out his fifteen-year-old girlfriend was pregnant, but not before slapping her around, yelling, "That ain't my kid." Angel had shoved him into the hallway, slammed the door in his face. She didn't want him. She didn't need him.

Two years after Jose was born, her mother died. Angel was seventeen. She almost buckled from the pressure of the responsibility to care for another, tiny human. She had no safety net. His dark eyes, staring up at her with such adoration . . . She'd shoved steel into her spine, stood up straight, and vowed her boy would be safe, happy, and healthy on her watch.

And she was doing it.

In a few more weeks, she'd be done with nursing school and would take her final boards. She survived by putting her head down and pushing through, focused on getting them out of this decrepit apartment building filled with dust and screeching train brakes. She kept the rest of the world's bullshit at arm's length.

"Usted va a la escuela, muestran al mundo que las niñas puertorriqueñas no deben ser," Mama said. *You go to college, show the world Puerto Rican girls are not to be messed with.*

There was a small inheritance when she died. Angel used the money and grants and side jobs to pay for the student nursing program at Bronx Community College. But with a child, it wasn't easy. Her lab partners would compare notes on grinding sessions and Beyoncé's salty AF concerts while she wrote reminders to pick up diapers and

Goldfish crackers. Thank God for Gabriela—her Domini-can neighbor had bullied her way into their lives a few years ago, insisting on helping with Jose. "Auntie" Gabriela treated them like family.

Angel stooped and gathered her homework from the apartment floor. She'd been working on it since returning home from morning practicum rounds. The medical training taught her to recognize Jose's triggers and how to deal with the onset of an asthma attack, but, really, she needed a good-paying job. A nursing job.

"*Mi chiquito?*" she called out. She and Jose had exchanged less than ten words that day, which had included *Can you keep it down? I've got to study.* As she scrabbled for air beneath an avalanche of schoolwork and practicums and part-time jobs, he got the short end of the stick.

She looked at the clock and the guilt bubbled up in her stomach. *How can it be time to go to work already?* She hated her nights at the Peacock. Her teeth clenched at the thought of the handsy men in their tailored suits and the entitled women with their eyes focused on the air above her forehead while they ordered their lavender-infused martinis. It took all her willpower not to throw the shade right back in their faces, with force. But the tips at the high-end club were too good. *Those bitches and their flowery drinks pay my rent.*

There was a knock at the door. Gabriela had come to get Jose and bring him with her downstairs, so he could hang out with her and the other stylists in Gabriela's beauty salon while Angel catered to the rich.

"Come in!" she shouted, and made her way back to Jose's room, picking up socks and a baseball mitt along the way. She pushed open his door, "Baby, how many times do I need to tell you to—"

Her heart lurched.

"Jose!"

Chapter Two

The student nurse at the local medical clinic's intake desk scrunched up her pink face as Angel glared at her. She and Angel were both in their early twenties, and in the same classes, but Theresa was routinely mistaken for a high school candy striper fresh from cheerleading practice.

"Angel, you know as well as I—"

"Look here, girl, you've got eyes in your head. Get the doctor. Now!" Angel gestured at the small boy huddled on Gabriela's lap in the waiting room, ashen-faced, with big, scared eyes, laboring to catch his breath.

Jose's face was only slightly more alert than when she'd found him a few minutes before, lying on his bedroom floor, gasping, the skin around his lips blue. His inhaler had been lying next to him. Empty.

I should have known it was empty. This is my fault. The rage, at herself and the world, roared through her like an apocalyptic fire.

From across the crowded room, she and Gabriela exchanged a glance. The older woman gave her a nod, agreeing with the young mother that it was time to release the mama bear.

Angel walked around the desk and loomed over her fellow student nurse, using her slim five-foot-eight frame to intimidate the even smaller girl. "Theresa, I am going back there. I'm not gonna spaz, I promise." *Sorry, that's bullshit,* she seethed. Turning and jogging down the hall before Theresa could gather her wits, she thought, *People don't start moving their asses, shit will burn.*

An X-ray tech and a registered nurse were walking toward her. "Hi," the RN said politely, but they didn't stop. Angel wore scrubs from her morning rounds. She blended right in.

She knew the nurse, and these rooms, not just because Jose was a repeat guest but also because this was where she'd been placed for her nursing practicum, with Dr. Collins as her supervisor.

She could hear the doctor's stupid, fake southern accent two doors away, followed by a nervous giggle. Walking past the open door, she could see the crusty bourgeois bastard, his signature black turtleneck setting off his waxy, pale flesh. He stood way too close to a teenage girl lying stiffly on the exam bed.

Angel coughed to get Dr. Collins's attention. *Where is the nurse who's supposed to be in here?*

"Hey! I didn't know you were on rounds tonight!" The doctor slid away from the teen, slicked back his silver hair. "We're waiting for Brandi's mom to come back with her paperwork."

Angel purposefully stepped closer to the exam table, forcing the doctor to slide further away. "Sorry to interrupt," she said blandly. "I'm not working, just checking to see where you're at with patients."

"The nurse can finish up here. I have a minute." Dr. Collins placed a hand on Angel's upper arm. Her muscle twitched involuntarily, his touch lingering too long, with a hint of a caress, before he casually dropped his hand and shoved it into the pocket of his lab coat. "Did you need something, darlin'? Help with one of your reports? We can go to my office . . ."

"No! No, sorry, it's Jose. He needs a breathing treatment. Right now. He's in distress."

"Ah. Sounds like it's time to get him on daily doses. Why don't you put him in exam room three. I'll meet you there in a minute," Dr. Collins drawled, raking his eyes up and down her body, settling on her chest. Even when she wore loose scrubs, the man had the ability to make her feel naked.

"Okay, but right away." She wanted to jam her fist down his throat, grab him by his goddamn phony Colonel Sanders vocal cords, and swing him around the room. It made her stomach roll to let him get away with his creep-ass behavior, but she only had to put up with the pig for a few more weeks. Once he signed off on her practicum, she planned to turn him into bacon.

Besides, he was the only one who could help her son right now. Keeping her lips pressed firmly together, Angel nodded and quickly retraced her steps to the waiting room.

Jose had been a healthy baby. Then, last year, he got pneumonia. Since then, he'd complained of an occasional tightening in his chest and start to wheeze. But a single puff from his inhaler had always solved it. *Today is different. I need Dr. Collins to fix this.* Through the open doors, she saw Jose sitting slumped in a chair. Her heart quailed. *Even if that means selling my soul.*

Gabriela was nowhere in sight. But there *was* a lanky man wearing sweats and a baseball cap, next to her son, talking to him. She hurried across the room.

"You like baseball, huh? You on a team?" The man's voice was mellow, the brim of his cap angled low. He was around her age and vaguely familiar. *Is he the water delivery guy?*

"Yeah." Jose sat up straighter as she approached, but his eyes were foggy, his voice rough and far away.

"What position do you play?"

"I like . . ." Jose took in a slow, agonizing breath, a tiny hand pressed against his chest, "shortstop."

"Easy, buddy. In . . . out . . . good. Shortstop is a great position. Very important to the team. With those long arms, I bet you get a lot of those grounders, huh?" When he realized someone was standing over them, the man glanced up.

Angel startled. From under the bill of his baseball cap, he peered at her with sharp, translucent eyes, a surprising green against his warm mahogany skin. He had high cheekbones and his lips were sculpted perfection. *Maybe I've seen him on a billboard?*

He broke their locked gaze, furrowing his brow at Jose as he struggled to answer the man's question.

The seven-year-old shut his eyes. "Yeah." Big, shallow breath. "I'm mad fast." Ragged cough.

"Jose," she said, upset with herself for getting side-tracked, even for a second. She gently drew the boy to his feet. He had deep, dark circles under his eyes. She pulled down his bottom eyelid; the color was faint but not gone. His breathing, however, sounded like a train from one of his cartoons. "Come on, *chiquito*, we've got an exam room ready."

"You be strong, little buddy." With graceful, fluid movements, the man bent over to retrieve a baseball that had fallen from Jose's lap when he stood. He slid the ball into the boy's sweatshirt pocket. "You don't want to forget this."

Jose nodded listlessly. The man patted his shoulder and then arched an eyebrow at Angel. "I'm not sure I should let you take off with this kid. Shouldn't you wait for his mom?"

Angel's mouth dropped open in surprise, but before she could retort, Gabriela materialized, flapping her hands anxiously.

"Finally! Thank the Lord!" The stylist kissed the top of Jose's head, then she batted her fake eyelashes and flipped around her long, shiny black hair, focusing in on Jose's new protector.

"Gabriela, you left him? With a stranger?" Angel asked through gritted teeth, keeping her eyes averted from those piercing green eyes while maneuvering Jose out from the adult bodies encircling him.

"Oh, honey, relax. Nursey over there was watchin' him. I had to use the ladies' room." Gabriela put her hands on her hips. "Besides, don't you know who this is?"

The man took a sudden step back, his eyes wide. Angel, her arm wrapped around Jose, was already moving her sick son toward the back hall. She couldn't care less about some hood rat, no matter how attractive. "There's an exam room ready. I'm taking him back." Guiding him past the chairs packed with coughing, groaning patients, Jose's ragged breathing distracting her, she said over her shoulder, "We'll be out soon, thanks."

"I'll be right here!" Gabriela shouted behind her.

Then she heard the green-eyed man say, "You gonna let a nurse talk to you like that?"

Her friend's response was smooth as Chanel silk and

filled the room. "And how the hell do you know she's not a doctor?"

Angel smiled without turning around. Gabriela always knew what to say.

Chapter Three

"Doc, you can't say anything. You gotta swear to that."

"Obviously. Besides, the muscles are just weak, you're going to be fine. Take it easy." Dr. Collins stood up, placed the extra tape and gauze on the counter. "Alright, you can put your sock and shoe back on. The nurse will bring your paperwork."

"No paperwork." Duke tasted iron. It was from biting his tongue. *This skinny motherfucker is a piece of work. I could knock him over if I blew on him.*

"Right." The doctor nodded, once, scrunching his black turtleneck. "Cash only, then." The exam room door swung shut behind the old white guy with the weird accent.

The ballplayer could only hope a newspaper didn't find out he'd been to the clinic. What if they offered the doc more money for details? The man was as smarmy as they came.

Duke took a deep breath, hopped off the table, and gingerly put his wrapped right foot on the ground. His green eyes narrowed to slits. While it was not unbearable, there was pain. And where there was pain, there was a problem.

When is this going to be done?

It wasn't just the ache. The unhealed ankle was a constant reminder of the worst night of Duke's life. In his dreams, he saw his friend Mark, the Bronx Bolt catcher, take a bullet in the chest, dying painfully fifty feet from him. Another stray bullet took Duke in the ankle but had seemed like nothing in comparison, until the wound put his career in jeopardy. Without baseball, he was nobody. Just another Bronx dude on the street, good for nothing but throwing a ball.

Caleb "the Duke" Lewis would be stripped of his status if he couldn't stand steady on the mound by the time he reported to spring training next week. The Bronx Bolts would replace him with the young buck they had waiting in the wings. Which was why he, the Bronx Bolts' star pitcher, was at a crappy clinic in the middle of the Bronx instead of at the Bronx Bolts' medical facility. He had to trust the skeezy Dr. Collins to keep his mouth shut.

In the waiting room, he found Aaron Miller, his agent and childhood friend, ranting into a cell phone, oblivious to the annoyed scowls from the people around him. Catching Duke's eye, Aaron clicked off and loped over.

"Man, you look fine. You're not even limping. You okay?"

"Yes." No.

"Good! Anyone recognize you?"

Duke tugged the brim of his baseball cap lower and shook his head. There was the mother in the waiting room earlier, but she hadn't taken any pictures. Maybe the sexy nurse—the uptight one who'd taken the asthmatic kid away . . . But he didn't think so.

There was something about that feisty young nurse. When their eyes had met, he'd felt a weird jolt, and now he couldn't stop thinking about her. The gold flecks in her brown eyes were mesmerizing, her skin was golden and smooth, her thick dark hair had gold highlights. She was naturally beautiful. *God musta sprinkled gold dust over that luscious woman.*

He turned to scan the room but then abruptly swung back around. *What am I thinking? I have got to get my shit together. No time to chase skirt around.*

"Yo, Earth to Duke. Let's get you outta here."

"Hang on, I gotta make a call." Walking out to Aaron's SUV, Duke tried calling his father, who was his business manager, but there was no response. "Pops," Duke said, leaving a message. "Call if you get this. I need you to drop some money at the clinic out in Mount Eden. I'll explain tonight." *And I don't need any of your bullshit,* he wanted to add, but didn't. He'd deal with his father later.

Aaron opened the car door for him, bowing like a butler. "Where you want to go, bro?"

"There's a bar a couple blocks from here." Duke pictured a row of tequila shots.

"We not going to some whack dive bar."

"Fine. Let's go to that place Roland's always talking about, not too far from here. The Peacock."

"And then I'm supposed to drive you home? From Mount Eden to Fordham? How is it I'm always the designated driver?"

"I'll take an Uber, you big fat baby." Duke smiled, knowing his agent would never allow him in a stranger's car. He was not going to let his star player out of his sight, not until Duke was safely back with the team. "Come on."

Angel had to leave the pharmacy before she found herself on the five o'clock news, wanted for murder.

The squat woman at the counter had tried to help, but after wrestling with the computer for a couple of minutes she told Angel, "Ma'am, your insurance is declining this prescription. They say they don't cover this medication."

"They covered it two weeks ago!"

"I'm sorry, ma'am, there's nothing I can do."

"Fine. How much is it?"

"The albuterol and inhaler are sixty dollars, if you get the one with only twenty doses. But the doctor wanted you to get the sixty-five-dose inhaler, plus a backup inhaler, and some Claritin." The counterwoman waited while Angel, cursing, dug out her wallet. She had just enough money for the small inhaler.

She pounded her thigh in frustration, guilt, and the unending river of anger. Dr. Collins had said Jose was completely recovered and that it was fine to send him home with Gabriela, that the treatment he had given the boy should last until tomorrow. *Should.*

She'd get Claritin after work, with her tips. And she'd bleach down the apartment walls again. Something was making his asthma worse. She'd been arguing with the landlord about the mold in the apartment for almost a year. He couldn't care less. For now, she could only clean and hope Jose didn't have another attack.

Out on the sidewalk, she shoved the medication in her bag, struggling not to tear up. *Not going to be buying groceries this week.* By the time she reached the Peacock, her blood hummed with angry electricity. In her head, she had created a script for the phone conversation she would have with her insurance company. There would be crying and pleading, but not from her. She was going to put the fear of God into those greedy bastards.

She leaned against the cement back wall of the club, tugged off her Adidas, and put on the high heels she had in her backpack. Then she sucked in her breath in order to bend over and tighten the heel straps, the button on her black skinny jeans gouging into her stomach.

A wolf whistle rang out from behind her. "Nice ass, mami," shouted a city worker. His partner added, "And those titties is bangin'!"

Angel straightened up. She decided there was no reason to stay calm. "You talk to your blow-up doll with that mouth?" she yelled at the orange-vested men. "Assholes!"

Oh, that felt gooood.

They hooted, and would have said more, if the side door to the Peacock hadn't popped open. The bouncer blocked out the light from the inside. "These guys bothering you?"

"No, I'm good, big man, thanks."

He offered the two morons a death stare and moved aside so she could enter. "Maybe not so good, Angel. You're late. Frank isn't happy."

She hurried down the hallway, fluorescent panels flickering overhead, her heels clicking on the concrete floor. Flinging open the office door, she was intent on clocking in.

She almost didn't see the skinny, pumping ass of her boss, or the hostess bent over the desk in front of him.

"You're! So! Big!" The woman's voice was disturbingly high-pitched and childlike. "Harder!" she squealed. Each thrust shoved her and the big metal desk across the floor.

"Yeah, yeah, like that," Frank said, clenching his hairy

butt cheeks, driving in and out of the hostess like a misfiring piston, neither of them aware of her.

Oh. My. God. He's not gay?

Angel, holding her breath, plucked her time card out of the slot and gently, oh so gently, slid it into the clock. Unfortunately, pushing the button slowly did nothing to soften the *click-click-click* of the time stamp.

Gripping the hips of the waitress for balance, Frank twisted to see who was behind him. He flashed a grin, his teeth a beacon of light in the dim room. "Angel! Want in on this?"

"I'm good, thanks," Angel said, backing out the door. The room had not been dim enough.

The hostess moaned, not bothering to turn around. "Don't stop! Don't stop!"

Angel let the door slam behind her. *I did not just see that. I did not just see that.* She focused on breathing, in and out. *Peace. Namaste. Baby kitties.* Then she threw back her shoulders. She did not have space in her head to deal with that crazy scene. Angel pushed the mess into a dark corner of her mind, shook her head, fluffed her ponytail. *Baby needs a new pair of shoes.*

Lastly, she plumped up her cleavage. If everyone was going to leer at the twins, might as well put the girls to work. Her uniform, besides the high heels and skinny jeans, was a purposefully ripped tank top that screamed "The Peacock" across the breasts.

Frank, who usually had tight white pants covering his

ass and wore a red velvet blazer, thought it was hilarious, his employees dressed in glam rock trash while serving forty-five-dollar apps to Richie Rich. The hipster customers liked it, thinking the owner was being ironic. The Wall Streeters liked it because they thought it was intended to mock the poor. And the letches liked it because the tanks were an easy window to the mandatory push-up bra.

The hostess was the only one who didn't have to wear the cheesy top, because, apparently, she was willing to wear nothing at all.

"You're late!" One of the many anorexic blonde servers yelled over the top of the loud house music, gesturing to the long list of drink orders sitting on the back bar.

"Yeah? The boss didn't have a problem with it."

A cougar dressed in Prada reached over the bar and waved a hand between Angel and the other bartender. "Hey, you," she said from between pouty duck lips. "Make me a Moscow mule."

"Can't you see we were talking—"

The other bartender interrupted Angel. "Can I suggest using our new gin, the Nolet's Silver, instead of the well liquor?" She gave Angel a quick glare as she held up the bottle.

The middle-aged woman tapped a Day-Glo orange nail on the bar. "Why are you asking me? Isn't that your job, to know how to make cocktails?"

Angel didn't bother telling either of them Moscow mules were made from vodka; instead, she turned her back and grabbed a knife. Hacking limes into wedges, she swallowed hard, choking on a lump of anger that had been growing since that morning and didn't look to be dissolving anytime soon.

It had been a long day. It was going to be a long night.

Chapter Four

Aaron got them a table in a dark corner of the club, which annoyed the hell out of Duke.

The ballplayer dropped onto one of the couches. He started to take off his hat, but Aaron put a hand on him, saying, "Keep that on."

Duke leaned back with his hands behind his head and stared down his agent.

Aaron rolled his eyes. "Seriously, man, I'm here to keep you out of trouble. The GM doesn't want to hear your name until roll call next week."

He can go fuck himself, Duke thought, though he didn't really have a beef with the general manager. When Duke was in trouble last year, the GM had his back, promising him his spot on the roster this spring—if his ankle was healed and there were no more scandals.

While logically he knew he had to lay low and stay out

of the public eye, he was getting frustrated with hiding away. It had felt good earlier that day, standing on the mound at the charity game, getting to do what he loved, out in the light of day. He hoped the doc was right, that the ankle was okay, just needed time to toughen up. *My God, what if I'm not ready next week?* His heart was in his stomach.

He caught a server's eye. *I can't do anything about it right now.* He stretched out, putting his feet on the low table. The ankle twinged, but only for a second.

"What'll you have?" a stick-thin blonde asked, bending low so her tank top exposed a lacy Victoria's Secret bra.

Ain't nothing to see on your skinny ass, girl, thought Duke.

Aaron felt differently, obviously, grilling her breasts. "I want a Manhattan. With those good cherries, none of that maraschino shit."

"And your best bottle of tequila, ASAP," a deep voice rolled out behind them. A tall, dark, black man layered in Armani stepped into their circle of low, overstuffed couches.

"Roland! What up?"

"Came to celebrate my retirement with you douche bags. And the Duke's new season. Let's go, girl. Get us some shots up in here." The towering, ebony-skinned man slapped the woman's ass, but she didn't seem to mind. It was Roland Smith. The people of New York loved him. He had been the flashy first baseman of the Bronx Bolts for years, batting as a lefty and coming close to Ty Cobb's record. Then, last year, the thirty-six-year-old hit a grand slam, ran through home, with the crowd going crazy, and tore the ligaments in his wrist. The nerve damage was irreparable. Time to hang up the baseball hat.

"Good to see you, brother. How'd you know we were here?"

"Talked to your pops. He said to say he sorry he missed you but he'll catch you later."

Duke snorted. "He been dodging me all week. I thought maybe he moved out but forgot to tell me." He peered around. "Where's Kinley? You leave the ol' lady at home?"

"Kinley at the movies with her girlfriends."

"Complaining about what a dick you are?"

"Bragging on my big dick." Roland folded his long body onto the cushion next to him. "How you doin', man? How's the ankle?" He dropped a hand on Duke's shoulder. "How's . . . everything?"

Duke coughed, to give himself a second. Roland had been with Duke and Mark the night of the shoot-out. Duke's girlfriend at the time, Regina, had also been there.

They'd been in a Chicago club, after a game. Roland was in the bathroom when a fight broke out between local gangbangers. Suddenly, everybody seemed to be shooting. Duke, standing at the bar, turned to see his girlfriend slide under a table, but then he took a bullet in the ankle before throwing himself behind another table.

Mark, his teammate, was not so lucky. He was shot in the chest, killed in the cross fire.

Roland *was* lucky, able to slip out a back door when the guns started going off. He didn't get hurt—and the first baseman managed to stay out of the limelight, with neither the police nor the press knowing he'd been there.

Duke, on the other hand, became part of a publicity nightmare for the Bronx Bolts. They'd lost their catcher in the high-profile crime, and their pitcher was injured, possibly involved in the carnage. Duke was quickly cleared of charges, but the media coverage was intense, and rarely pretty. He fell into a dark depression, dealing with the loss of his friend while also healing physically. The bullet had torn through ligaments and muscles, keeping Duke off his feet. He could do nothing but sit and stew. And drink.

He dwelled on Mark's death and started partying like it was a job. Which led to a very ugly public breakup with Regina, who refused to discuss what she called "the past." Her modeling career had jumped tiers and she had no patience for a drunk invalid.

The Bronx Bolts' manager called Duke to the clubhouse. Skip told him to clean up his act if he wanted to play again. Then the Bronx Bolts management told Duke's agent he'd best keep an eye on his number one meal ticket or both Duke and Aaron would be out. To drive the point home, the Bronx Bolts drafted another pitcher . . . Just in case, they said.

Hiding in the corner of the Peacock now, Duke felt it had been long enough. It was time to shake off the darkness and get back to the game. He was tired of being depressed. He wanted his old life back.

"Eh, the ankle's fine. Good as new. Can't wait to get to training." Duke grabbed the tequila shot as it arrived, taking the bottle and putting it in front of him. "And here's to Mark, may he rest in peace."

They clinked glasses.

"Hey," Aaron said, moving the bottle away from Duke. "Did you see they finally found those Chi-town thug-heads guilty?"

Duke frowned. The trial had dragged on so long because everyone believed there was a missing shooter— they'd never found the gun that killed Mark. His friend's murderer was probably still out there.

"I don't want to talk about it. And quit trying to play my nursemaid, Aaron. I got this. I'm not going to make a fool of myself." Duke slugged back his drink and reached for the bottle, refilling his glass.

"You go down, I go down."

"Dude, chill out. No one knows we're here. It's fine."

Roland butted in. "Dude, what happened with the ugly finder you pitched today? Anyone get hurt?"

"What's an ugly finder?" asked Aaron.

Duke grinned. "The foul ball that moron hit into the dugout today, that's called an ugly finder. The ball will either find someone who is ugly or make him that way, if he gets hit. In this case, Johnny B took one on his big fore-head. Luckily, he didn't have any looks to worry about."

"Goddamn, I wish I'd seen it! I bet he cried like a baby." Roland hooted with laughter. "Too bad it didn't hit that bastard harder—coulda knocked the ugly right off him. An ugly finder . . . perfect!"

A server walked up just then, her back to Duke as she slammed down a tray with glasses of water and a bowl of house-made chips. He heard her snort and then say to Roland, "You're talking about that poor player who got hit in the dugout today? Nice."

She stalked off before they could respond. Something about her walk and the swing of her curly ponytail was familiar. *Do I know her?* thought Duke. *Hard to tell*, he decided. He knew so many bitchy girls.

A few more tequila shots and, soon enough, Duke's ankle no longer mattered and the images of Mark, lying in a pool of blood, faded into the background.

The three men drank and riffed on each other and sized up the women.

Roland suddenly perked up. "Hey, I think I recognize that lippy bartender. I think she's a stripper at that new place over on Bronx Street." He pointed toward the end of the bar. "She has one helluva ass. And she does this thing where she grabs a beer and pours it out, real slow, over her white T-shirt. Hot."

Aaron leaned forward and tilted his head, judging. "I wouldn't mind seeing that."

Duke pushed up the brim of his hat and turned to take a closer look.

He could see her face now. It was the nurse from earlier today. She was the bartender.

He tugged his lid back down. If he was smart, he'd leave. She probably knew who he was by now. He didn't need a bartender calling up the news stations.

But, my God, she is beautiful. If she did work a pole, the place had to be top-notch. Even with her long, kinky hair pulled back into a ponytail and no makeup on, she was way sexier than any of the glitzy, fake women filling the room with their expensive perfume and shrieky laughter.

He stood up, swaying. "I'm gonna go say hi. Hold my beer."

"You don't have a beer."

Angel worked hard at keeping a pleasant expression on her face while filling drink orders. Even when she had to deliver the drinks out to the floor herself because the servers were busy flirting with married men, she remained pleasant. Even when each drink came with special instructions—"Oh, shaken, not stirred, and shaken at least sixty-five times, thanks"—she kept a smile on her face.

The boss sidled up to her behind the bar with a smirk. He was no longer naked, now wearing a tight white T-shirt under his red velvet jacket, making his spray tan even darker. And oranger.

She wanted to hose him down with club soda, but she

filled the glasses instead, proud of her restraint. "You are a disgusting human being."

He laughed, white teeth blinding her, and put an arm around her shoulders. "You need to loosen up."

"Get the fuck away from me, Frank, or you're going to lose a hand."

"Spunky, spunky." He moved back, shrugged. "Your loss. Listen, I'm gonna have you come in early the next coupla nights, create more specialty craft cocktails for the drink menu and practice some new techniques. No more bruising the ice. Stir, don't shake. And I've come up with a signature drink, the Bronx Boulevardier. You're going to premix and age it in these charred oak barrels." He caressed a couple of small casks on the back bar, which were taking up the prep space.

Oh, good. So we can be like every other lounge in town, serving Manhattans out of cute little barrels. "You know I can't be here early. I have my finals coming up, plus I've got Jose."

"You're a mixologist at the Peacock. There are plenty of girls who'd give their left tit for your job."

"Uh-huh." No way was he going to fire his only POC. She'd sue him for racism—and sexual harassment—and he knew it. "Well, we'll have to talk about this later. I've got to get these drinks out." It was enough that she had to keep her mouth shut around Dr. Collins; she wasn't about to let a hipster-bar owner treat her like crap. *And "mixologist"? Please. These girls aren't career bartenders.* No one at the Peacock was studying the craft or science of mixing drinks; they might throw around buzzwords like *muddle* or *artisanal bitters* and put on a good show with the copper shakers, but they were here to snag a drunk, rich boyfriend.

A few minutes later, she was brewing up a row of old-fashioneds but going over nursing notes in her head, picturing the steps necessary to insert a PICC line—a tiny, flexible tube running from the arm into the chest to serve as a heart catheter—when someone leaned across the bar and interrupted her concentration. "Hey," a man said. Then, louder, "Hey there."

She could hear the drunken tinge. "Yeah, hold on a sec."

Then a hand reached across the bar and tapped her shoulder, hard. "I hear you take off your shirt for tips. Is that true? You one fine stripper."

She snapped.

"Take your fucking hands off me!" she bellowed.

And, without thinking, she threw an old-fashioned in the man's face.

Oh shit, she thought, shocked by her loss of control.

"Goddamn!" the man shouted, hundred-proof bourbon streaming off the bill of his baseball cap and down his neck. He flipped off the hat with a shake, an orange twist falling on the bar between them. Even with drooping eyelids, his eyes were an unmistakable shade of green.

"You!"

Swiping at the wet on his shirt, he grimaced. "Yeah, me."

"I, I—" She was trying to decide if her fury was justified with the lit piece of man meat in front of her or if she'd possibly overreacted. "I'm sorry. I—"

"What is this?" Frank charged toward them, his velvet blazer flapping. "I am so sorry, sir! This will be taken care of immediately. Your drinks are covered tonight, on the house."

"Looks more like they're on me," the man said.

Frank caught the man's eye and turned chalk white. He gulped and turned to Angel. "Get out. You're fired. And this is coming out of your pay."

"But—"

"Angel, leave. Now."

"You're an asshole, Frank!" She threw a hate-filled glare at him and then at the green-eyed man, who stood emotionless, his face blank.

Frank yelled after her as she stormed out the door, but she wasn't listening. She was done listening to men.

Chapter Five

So, that happened.

By the time she got back to her apartment building, with the streetlights coming on around her and the construction workers done hammering for the night, she'd calmed down. Regret had replaced rage. She'd couldn't afford to let her temper get loose. Jose couldn't afford her mistake. *Oh my God, the Claritin.* Hopefully, he'd be okay for the night. She'd have to beg Frank for her job back. Her stomach turned to lead. She shouldn't have to grovel, ever, but especially when she'd just been sticking up for herself. *So unfair.*

The lights were on in Gabriela's salon, on the ground floor below her apartment. Surprised, Angel pushed open the doors.

"Hey, how come you're still open?"

A row of women and her son turned to her.

Gabriela, tugging rollers from the hair of an older woman in her chair, asked, "What do you mean? Why you home so early? It's only six."

Angel checked her phone. Her body was so fatigued, it could have been midnight. She flicked her eyes at Jose, who sat in a chair at Latisha's station, and said, "Uh, Frank let me go early. How about you, baby? You feeling okay?"

"I'm good, Mama. My chest still kinda hurts, but not bad." Angel dropped to her knees in front of him, worried, but he went on in a happy rush, "Auntie Gabriela and Auntie Latisha are gonna put my team colors in my hair!"

The boy, small for his age, had a black apron draped over him, his scrawny arms sticking out, clutching one of the kid magazines Gabriela kept around for him.

"Oh, really? Yellow and purple?" She narrowed her eyes at Latisha as she stood back up. "I'm assuming this was your idea?"

"What our baby wants, our baby gets," Latisha crooned, running her fingernails, painted with leopard print, through Jose's tightly curled hair, making him giggle. The seven-year-old was treated like the salon pet, and he loved it. He had more toys tucked away in the corner of the shop than he did in the apartment upstairs. Gabriela had even bought a small table and chair, so he could do his homework.

"Can I, Mama?"

"Oh, sure, now you ask my permission. It's late, chiquito. This is going to take forever."

"Mama! It's Saturday! I don't have school tomorrow."

Gabriela paused over her customer's head and said, "Girl, I will happily do something with your mop while that boy is getting worked on."

"Damn! There is nothing wrong with my hair! Besides, how would you know? I have to keep it back all the time."

"My point exactly. You blending into the woodwork. Let's throw some highlights up in there, give some shape to those frizzy-ass curls."

"My hair is not frizzy."

"Are you sure about that? When *was* the last time you wore it down, gave yourself a little love?"

Latisha cackled. "She givin' herself love, alright—she ain't been letting no man in there."

Angel flashed at her. "Seriously? You gotta do that in front of him?"

Jose looked up from his *Sports Illustrated for Kids*. "What?"

Latisha spun him around until he giggled again. "Your ma's just being touchy. She jealous because we workin' on you and not her."

"I wouldn't let you touch me with a ten-foot pole, Latisha."

"As long as you're letting someone's pole touch you, honey. You cranky, need to take care of business."

"Oh my God. Shut up."

The women were laughing and offering more undesired dating advice as she dropped into an empty chair with her backpack and tugged out her books. "Fine, you can do Jose's hair. I can use the time to study."

Their voices melded into white noise as she fell back into her anatomy textbook, once again studying the internal workings of the human sex organs. Briefly, she pictured herself lining up the men she'd encountered that day and kicking each one squarely in the testes. A satisfying image at first, until she realized her anger had only managed to get her into hot water—it certainly hadn't solved any of her problems. Getting her nursing license was the only thing that could do that.

She turned to the next section in the book, determined to move forward, to be better. To be there for her son so he didn't die.

"I cannot believe one of my employees would do that to you—I mean you, the Duke!" The owner of the Peacock trailed off, wringing his hands. "Like I said, do not worry about your bill. It's taken care of. I just can't apologize enough—"

"Dude, I am not making a server pay my tab. I was rude to her. I deserved it. Now, take my card." Duke thrust his Visa into the owner's hands.

Roland and Aaron, with two women in short shorts sandwiched between them, laughed. The ex-ballplayer said, "Idiot. Let them foot the bill."

"Nah, I got this." Duke was miserable. He had sobered

up quickly when he realized he'd caused the bartender to lose her job. *If she's working at the clinic and working at a bar, she must need the money.* "I feel like a total dick."

"C'mon, you were hitting on her. She should be used to it. She's fucking dressed like a tramp. Obviously she wants the attention."

"She's no thot. That nurse is sexy as hell."

Roland hunched his shoulders. "Nurse? We're in a club, homey."

"I saw her earlier today. She's a nurse at the clinic."

His agent tuned in. "Wait, you saw her earlier? The bartender who just blasted you?" Aaron's voice dropped in pitch. He fluttered his hand at the whispering girls on the couch with them. "Ladies, can you excuse us?"

Miffed, they sauntered away. Roland watched them go, puzzled, then said, "What clinic? Why were you at a clinic?"

Aaron talked over him. "Does she know who you are? Duke, if she tells anyone you've hurt your ankle, the GM is gonna find out."

"I thought your ankle was healed," Roland said.

"No, she doesn't know who I am, and no, my ankle is fine, like I told you. I kinda tweaked it at the charity game earlier, but, seriously, it doesn't hurt now."

"How do you know she doesn't recognize you?"

"Come on. If she did, she'd have said something. Or tried to sue me instead of throwing a drink on me." *My stupid ass got lucky. While she got fired.* He cringed.

"Well, let's get outta here. I'll drop you at your place."

The owner materialized at the foot of the couch. "Um, Duke, sir, I think we need to run another card. I'm really sorry, this one has been declined."

"No way. Run it again."

"We ran it four times. I'm sorry. They want me to cut up the Visa. But I won't do that." He handed the card to a perplexed Duke, who let it hang limply between his fingers. He tried to exude cool and confidence, but he had a bad feeling. *What's going on?*

Roland slapped the table, loudly. "Well, it's a good thing this was on the house, am I right?" The tall ex-Bronx Bolt gave the owner a meaningful look.

"Yep. Yep, that is exactly what I was thinking. You boys have a nice night, and please, come again."

Chapter Six

"Mom. Mama."

"Hmm."

"Mama. Mama. Ma."

"What? I'm sleeping."

"I'm hungry."

"You can make toast. You have my permission." She drew the blanket over her head.

"I did. But it's smoking."

Angel threw back the comforter, tiny feathers erupting into a mushroom cloud, and ran to the kitchen.

After unplugging a flaming toaster and throwing it in the sink, she gave Jose a bowl of Tastee-O's, using the last of the milk on the cereal and adding a few shriveled blueberries. She settled for the remaining heel from the loaf of bread and a mug of reheated coffee.

While he ate, she sponged soot off the walls. She was

wiping dark streaks from the glass on a framed poster—
it was a cheap reproduction of the Puerto Rican painter
Botello's *Cabeza*—when she heard Jose sniffle and say, "I'm
sorry I got that on you, Mama."

She put the sponge down and picked him up, even
though he was too big for that, balancing him on her hip.
"What do you mean?"

"She looks like you. The pretty lady in the painting.
Auntie Gabriela thinks so, too. And now she's dirty."

"Oh, sheesh, it came right off. See?" They cocked their
heads to the same side, mother and son, studying the painting. The woman had high cheekbones, full lips, and gold
at the center of her broody cat eyes. *She looks like she's exhausted
and angry at the world, so, yeah.*

"You're prettier than she is."

Angel grinned at him. "Uh-huh, and what is it you
want, little man?"

"If I promise not to talk to you, will you stay home
today?"

Good mood: shredded.

"We've got a while before my rounds start. Let's
go cuddle in bed and read *Magic Tree House*, what do you
say?"

The aroma of the dark organic coffee steeping in the French
press filled the room. Duke leaned against the island range,
scrambling eggs and sausage. His mind repeatedly returned
to the gorgeous bartender from last night. *I need to make that*

right, he thought. He added chives and diced peppers and made the decision to find her and apologize.

"The Duke is making his own breakfast. Just like the little people."

"I always make my breakfast." The Bronx Bolt pitcher refused to let his father get to him. He stirred in goat cheese. "Where've you been, Pops? We've got things to talk about."

Willis Lewis poured himself a cup of coffee but didn't offer any to his son. Sitting at the long marble counter, he shook out the morning paper and said, "I'm a busy man. I'm running three different local commissions right now and planning a march for next month."

"Yeah, well, you supposed to be managing my money. Yet, last night, my credit card was declined."

Willis slowly turned a page, engrossed. "I'll look into it."

"That's all you've got to say? What's going on, Pops?"

The older man didn't answer at first, turning pages silently. Then, "Give it a rest. I paid the bill. Someone screwed up. It doesn't help, you so irresponsible with your spending."

Duke, irritated, scraped the eggs onto a single plate, not inclined to share his food after his father's jab. "I need some cash delivered to that clinic next to the WinCo in Mount Eden. The doc wants fifteen hundred."

Willis finally held the newspaper still. "What doctor? Why cash? Tell me you did not agree to pay for an abortion. The press—"

"Jesus, no. I haven't been with anyone since Regina. I had my ankle checked out and I didn't want anyone to make a big deal of it."

"But you're okay? You'll be able to report next week?"

"Yes."

"And Regina . . . You staying away from her?"

"Yes! What do you care?"

"You have bad taste in women. She was taking you for a ride."

Biting his tongue, Duke said, "Whatever. I gotta go. I'm going to take some money from the safe."

"Nah, I put it in the bank. I didn't like having that much cash in the house. I'll take care of it, son. I'll pay the bill this afternoon."

Duke looked at him sharply. "That's my money. Don't you think you should have talked to me first?"

Willis pushed back from the table and folded his arms. "You don't trust me?"

The question was loaded, and his father knew it. Duke's mother had left because of Willis's out-of-control gambling. It wasn't until a bookie showed up at Duke's high school, cornered the teen in the locker room, and punched him in the kidney three or four times, leaving Willis's son to piss blood, that his father finally got help, stopped drinking, and gave up gambling.

He'd changed over the years, becoming a leader in the community, though Willis never did get the hang of being a normal, caring father. He put his reputation and

random girlfriends first. But his father *was* a solid busi-
nessman, managing Duke's finances so he wouldn't end up
like other professional athletes who pissed away large sums
of money. Well, solid until recently, anyway. Duke was
suddenly receiving late notices from bill collectors. Willis
was off his game.

Duke prayed he wasn't gambling again. "Don't play
the guilt card. I agreed to let you be my manager as long
as you keep things transparent. You might have the best
intentions, and God knows you're good at making a dol-
lar, but you're also an addict."

"Your faith in me is hardly overwhelming." Willis took
a swig of coffee, picking up another newspaper. "Try looking in a mirror. You went crazy, remember? You burned
through a lot of money with your partying and your legal
bullshit. I'm the one who made sure you stayed afloat."

"Just fix the credit card and pay the clinic, okay?"

"Yes, m'lord."

Duke slammed out the back door, leaving his breakfast behind. His father had pulled so much crap over the
years, and yet Duke had given him chance after chance.
Willis resembled Duke in many ways, with his deep mahogany cast, green eyes, and lithe build. But the old man
also had leathery skin, yellowed whites in his eyes, a hard
potbelly, and the ability to forget Duke was family. If only
Willis would show a little gratitude. Maybe even treat him
like a son.

•   •   •

Angel counted to ten, staring at the ceiling tiles in the back hallway of the clinic, slowly inhaling antiseptic and urine smells and exhaling frustration. *Mama always taught me to stop and think before reacting.*

Her mama's advice was keeping Dr. Collins alive—Angel sat at the nurse's station, filling out charts and plotting the man's death, but the "Do unto others" mantra Mama had drilled into her now guilted her into restraining her crazy. Trying to complete a form, she broke the lead of an automatic pencil for the third time and cursed.

This was supposed to be her last shift at the clinic before she graduated, and Dr. Collins was supposed to sit down with her for a final exit interview at the end of the night's shift, so he could provide a recommendation for licensure. But, without talking to her, he'd just switched her schedule.

When she'd arrived, she found Theresa in front of the scheduling board, her shoulders slumped. "They just gave me extra shifts through next week," the nursing student from Angel's cohort said. "I'm going to miss my mom's birthday party. And I need to study!" The last came out in a wail.

"That sucks . . ."

"It's not just me," the pink-faced girl sniffed. "You've got more shifts, too."

Peering at the board, Angel found her name. There

she was, scheduled for extra rounds, and Dr. Collins had pushed back the exit interview to next week.

She gave up on the charts and threw the automatic pencil across the desk. *Am I ever going to be in control?* Some women wanted a rich man to swoop in and carry them away to a royal palace where they would be dressed and bathed by servants, fanned with ostrich feathers, and fed grapes by heavily muscled men, never to be responsible for anything ever again. Not Angel. She didn't trust anyone else to fix her problems or make decisions that impacted her, and especially not any that affected Jose. *But it sure would be nice if asshats would get out of my way, let me get stuff done.*

Though, what would it be like to have someone take care of me, just once? . . . No. She couldn't let herself waver. *I need to put my head back down and keep working. I'm the one responsible for reaching the light in the tunnel,* she reminded herself.

By the end of her shift, she was beat. She had shadowed the RNs, drawing blood and giving shots to screaming children and apathetic old people with no veins. Then Dr. Collins had her assist as he picked dozens of large, creosote-soaked splinters from the inner arms of a utility worker. The burly guy's support strap had loosened and he'd slid down a twenty-foot telephone pole in less than two seconds. Sitting on the table, the big man allowed a few tears to slip out as the bigger pieces were tugged free, but he never uttered a sound, other than grinding his teeth. Angel admired his stoicism.

After clocking out, Angel walked toward the exit, exhausted and trying to smooth coils of dark hair back into her ponytail.

Dr. Collins came up behind her as she reached the doors. "You did great in there, darlin'." He gave her an awkward, one-armed hug, the gel in his hair glistening. "You're a natural, Angel. Stick with me, you're going places."

I don't want to stick with you, freak. Fill out my goddamn review! "Thank you, Dr. Collins. I've learned a lot from you."

"And how is your son?"

"He's doing better today. I couldn't buy a backup inhaler, though. My insurance has decided asthma is a preexisting condition. They don't have to cover his medicines."

"Why didn't you say so? Come here."

She followed him back down the hall, anxious, as he opened the locked room where the medications were stored. He went to a shelf and dug around until he found the box with the inhalers. He handed her one. "Here you go, sweetie. We can't have him suffering another attack, can we?" As she went to grab it, he held it back and regarded her intently. "Come to me whenever you need more."

She took the inhaler cautiously. "I can't give you anything for this."

His glance skittered across her chest and back up to her face. "No worries. I like to make sure my staff is taken care of."

She clutched the medicine to her chest, clamping her mouth down before she lashed out. The past few years, her temper had been like a stove burner that wouldn't switch off, usually on low but easily turned up, glowing red at the slightest provocation. No matter how much Dr. Collins deserved to be burned, she had to figure out a way to stay cool.

Theresa pushed through the door. "Oh, hey, we need some . . ." The pink-faced girl squinted at a paper in her hand. "Epinephrine. Can you help me, Angel?"

Dr. Collins winked at Angel and left. It would feel amazing to let him have it, but thank God she'd kept it together—it was more important that she provide for Jose.

Once the door swung shut, Theresa put down the slip of paper and said, "Whew. That was close. You're welcome."

"You interrupted us on purpose?"

"I don't like that guy. No one does."

Angel blew out a frustrated breath. "He gave me this sample. I'm hoping he doesn't think I owe him." The counter on the inhaler showed only six puffs. She zipped open her bag and slid the medicine inside.

The other girl pursed her lips. "Oh."

"I cannot wait to be free of this place."

Hoisting her backpack, she opened the door and poked her head out slowly, as if in a spy movie. The hall was empty. She strode out, relief setting in when she hit the waiting room.

Bursting out the double doors, into the weak February sun, she felt like an escapee from prison. At the bottom of the stairs, she closed her eyes and tilted her face to the light.

"That feels nice, don't it?"

Her eyelids popped open. A foot from her face were the amazing green eyes of the man who got her fired from the Peacock.

"Are you kidding me right now?"

The lanky, graceful man backpedaled. "That sounded like I was being creepy. The sun. I meant the sun feels good."

"Back off."

"Hey now."

"You were here yesterday, then at the club—and, by the way, thank you for that—and now here you are again. Are you stalking me?"

"No! Well, maybe, I guess, right now. I was trying to find you to apologize."

"Job well done." She edged away from him and started down the sidewalk.

"Come on, let me make it up to you."

"Stop following me."

"Did you get fired for real? I'll go back, talk to your boss."

"I don't need anything from you."

"I'm sorry. Now you're freaked out."

"It would help if you weren't tailing me."

He stopped. For a second she thought he'd finally gotten the hint, but then he was back at her side, this time holding out a couple of dandelions he'd picked from the sidewalk.

"Here."

"Yeah, this is a lot less creepy. Stalking *and* random gifts."

"I promise not to leave a boiling pet bunny on your stove."

She recoiled. "Uh . . . good?"

"Oh, shit. That's from a movie. You know, Sharon Stone? Hatin' on her man's wife, kills the family pet?"

"Seriously, get the hell away from me." She let her backpack drop down into her hand, so she was swinging it by the strap. A couple of textbooks upside the head would drop the motherfucker.

His face went hangdog, so filled with misery that she almost laughed.

"I have really screwed this up, haven't I? I'll leave you be." He tipped his baseball hat at her, turned around, and started to walk away. But then, midstride, he stopped. "Oh, I meant to ask, how is that boy? He okay?"

She narrowed her eyes. "Are you talking about Jose?"

"Maybe . . . The kid having a hard time breathing yesterday?"

"He's fine."

"That's good." He turned back around with a wave and started in the opposite direction.

Without thinking, she called after him, "That was nice, what you did with him in the waiting room. Talking to him, keeping him calm."

"I had asthma as a kid. It can be real scary. I hope his mama got his back."

Angel did a double take. "Of course I do," she yelled.

"What?" Twenty feet away, he paused, turned, and sized her up. "I thought you was the nurse."

"You can say it." She felt her blood pressure rise. "I'm too young to have a kid his age."

"Whoa, I ain't nobody's judge. You workin' two jobs, taking care of your boy, then you doin' right."

"I'd be working a whole lot more if it weren't for you."

"Lord, woman, we back on that?" He came closer. "I swear, I am sorry. But you were pretty outrageous your-self, am I right?"

"You thought I was a stripper!"

"I promise you, I did not. I knew you were the nurse from the clinic. I was drunk and trying to be funny."

She was quiet for a minute, replaying the drink in the face. She shook her head, offered a short laugh. "You should not disrespect women that way. But maybe I went too far. You were the straw that broke the camel's back. You would not believe the day I'd had."

"If it matters, my day wasn't that hot, either." He glanced down at her, the color of his eyes once again mak-ing her catch her breath. "So, tell me, what was so bad yesterday?"

"Are you asking me about my day? Wow. It's been a while since someone did that." *That's right. I don't have a boyfriend . . .*

"You're stalling."

"You wanna hear? Alright . . ." Angel felt the anger build up in her again as she thought about trying to balance working and studying, Jose's emergency, then Dr. Collins and his sliminess, then the insurance company refusing to pay for Jose's medicine . . .

As they walked, she unloaded on the poor man, a complete stranger. It didn't matter if the guy was listening or not, or even if he was there. By the time she got around to describing the catcallers and then Frank's office sexploits and him asking her to join in, she was spitting out her words, bullets of angst and frustration and not a little fear released into the air. Slowly, her chest felt lighter. "And, then, you asked me to take my shirt off."

"That's not exactly what I said."

She laughed. "I know. More than what you said, I think it was when you touched me that I lost it. You came into my space bubble."

They were walking along a chain-link fence next to a school. An older guy was yelling out commands to a group of boys practicing baseball on a small dirt infield. Angel hesitated and then said, "This is my stop. I guess we can chalk yesterday up to a full moon or something and forget about it, what do you say?"

"Shake on it." He thrust out his hand. "That is, if you'll let me invade your space bubble one last time."

She laughed again, shaking his hand. His grip was warm and firm and she didn't want him to let go.

"Is that your boy out there?"

"Jose. Yes. Gabriela, the neighbor you met yesterday, dropped him off for this baseball club. He's not interested in basketball. He and his friends live for baseball, spending the winter getting ready for the regular season."

"Again, I'm not judging, but I'm surprised you let him outside today."

She sighed. "I know. Believe me, I know. But I can't keep him locked up in our apartment. He loves baseball so much, it would kill him if I said no. They normally are inside anyway, doing what they can in the gym or batting cage, but it's hard to keep them cooped up when the weather is nice enough to be outside. The guy running the club knows what's going on and keeps a close eye on him. You'd be surprised how many kids on Jose's team have asthma."

"Looks like the coach could use a hand." With that, Duke skirted the fence and jogged over to the pudgy guy on the mound throwing pitches to the kids.

Lord, don't let him be a pedophile. She didn't get that vibe from him, but who knew? The coach must have been okay with it, though, handing him a glove and a ball and leaving the man on the mound. After only a minute, it was clear he was simply another kid on the field, in love with a game and wanting nothing more than to play ball. A big, handsome kid.

She realized she didn't know his name. Propping her elbows on the fence, she watched him stretching and moving like a jaguar, his chest muscles outlined by his T-shirt. *He's easy to look at, if nothing else.* Angel could hear the man call out directions and encouragement to the boys, firm but not condescending, as he sent them a variety of pitches. There was some heckling and some laughing, but mostly these kids were serious, intent on proving their worth.

One kid knocked back a pitch with a solid crack. The man leapt up with ease and plucked it out of the air, then threw the ball to the tiny catcher behind the plate so the boy could take out a player trying to make it home. The third baseman and the catcher had the tiny runner boxed in, but then fumbled the ball.

The man ran over to grab the ball rolling in his direction, but somehow ended up in the middle of a kid pileup. By the time they were untangled, the man laughed and called a time-out. He made his way to the dugout and the coach went back to the mound.

Angel started to step around the fence, but then decided not to interrupt when she saw the man dig a cell phone out of his pants pocket. He was immediately involved in a heated conversation, chopping and jabbing the air with his free hand. After he hung up, he spent a few more minutes talking to the kids on the bench, finally passing out high fives and fist bumps before walking back toward her.

That's when she noticed he was favoring his right leg. He tried to hide it, but his ankle clearly hurt him. *Must be why he was at the clinic yesterday.*

He reached her, winced, and then said, "Hey, I gotta go, but I told the coach I'd try to come back sometime, maybe help with batting practice." He took his hat off and caught her eye. He didn't look away. He was standing very close, close enough that she could feel the heat from his body. His breath on her cheek. For the first time, she noticed the freckles on his nose, and his long eyelashes. He smelled like apples. She wanted to bite him.

The air around them was charged. "You were good with them. And Jose yesterday . . ." she stammered.

"They're fun. And your Jose is a sweet kid. Just like his mama."

Spontaneously, Angel stood on tiptoes, tilted her head, and leaned in to him, meaning to give him a kiss on the cheek. Instead, her lips met his.

She should have backed away, but, oh, the zing that went up her spine, the warmth that flooded her stomach . . . His lips were so full and soft, moving under hers, the taste of salt and sex coming off him. Her lips parted, wanting to take him in, and her arms went up, trying to wind around his neck and bring him close.

Next to them, a car honked.

Abruptly, he pushed her away, though gently. His gaze was intense. She couldn't tell what fueled the burning green stare. Anger? Disgust?

Shame waved over her. *I attacked him! Again! What's wrong with me?*

A black Mercedes SUV sat at the curb. The window powered down and the driver, a guy dressed in an expensive suit and a loud tie, beckoned at the man she had kissed. The stranger who had rejected her. The blush spreading across her face felt like fire.

"Yo! Let's go!"

The man turned to Angel, a bemused grimace twisting his lips. "That's my agent."

"Get in the goddamn car! They're on their way!"

He limped over to the Mercedes and slid in without glancing back. Before she could say anything, the SUV peeled out into the street, causing several cars to slam on their breaks and honk.

What just happened?

Suddenly, she was surrounded by sweaty seven-year-olds who were jumping up and down, shouting and laughing.

Jose tugged on her shirt, a huge grin on his face. "Mama! Were you just kissing the Duke?"

"Who?"

Her son's jaw went slack with surprise and then delight. "That was the Duke!" He widened his stance and folded his arms, putting on his adult face. "It's okay, Mama. I didn't recognize him yesterday."

"The Duke?" It took her a second to place the name.

"Are you talking about the pitcher for the Bronx Bolts? That Duke?" Even as she was saying it, she knew it to be true. *Oh my God. How did I not recognize him?* She didn't follow baseball, but New Yorkers made sure everyone in the city knew the Bronx Bolts' roster. She was too busy to care about dudes famous for hitting balls with sticks and then whining about their mansions being too small.

I guess I should crawl out from under my rock more often. Then, after reflecting on the last few moments, she thought, *Better yet, I should get back under that rock and not come out.*

As she and Jose walked home, she shivered against the afternoon breeze blowing off the Harlem River. Everything felt dreamlike, unreal. Jose chattered away in the foreign language of baseball while she nodded absently and tried to calm the storm in her head. She wanted to lie down on the dirty sidewalk and cry. Twice now she'd given in to irrational impulses and stepped in it. And both lapses had involved this stranger, this Duke. A professional athlete, way out of her league.

The handsome, confident man had been normal, even friendly, once he got his foot out of his mouth. And her tongue. *Imagine being on a date with that guy. I bet we wouldn't go to Wendy's.* She frowned. *What's this "we" business? He ran away without asking my name.*

And it came to her. Why she had recognized his face. Not because he was a ballplayer but because his picture had been on the front page of the *Bronx Times* for weeks last year, something to do with getting shot in a bar, and one of his teammates had died. Also, didn't his agent-driver person just yell, *They're on their way?* Was he talking about the cops?

Thank God the guy left when he did. She'd dodged her own bullet. She did not have time for a man, but especially one who came with so much baggage and drama and who certainly saw her as a lesser being, from the wrong side of the tracks. She shivered again, this time not so much from the spring winds as from the goose that walked over her grave.

Yeah, how lucky. He didn't want me.

Chapter Seven

"Angel."

Her head snapped up when she heard her name. "I'm awake."

The day after kissing a Bronx Bolt at the park, she was back to sitting at the nurse's station, nodding off while trying to catch up on assigned reading: *Health Promotion in Multicultural Populations*, written by a bunch of white guys who'd clearly never left the Upper East Side.

"Uh-huh. I can tell. Can you take the patient in room four? Dr. Collins wants you to wrap an ankle." Theresa grinned. "You'll want this one. He's hot."

Angel grabbed the chart from Theresa's hands. "Caleb Lewis?"

The student nurse was already halfway down the hall, chasing an old man heading toward the bathroom with his gown wide open in the back.

Angel knocked on exam room four and pushed the door open. "Mr. Lewis?"

The man on the table was wearing a hoodie, his face obscured. When he shoved the hood back, the blood left her brain, leaving her dizzy. There, on her exam table, was the Duke.

"Caleb? You're Caleb Lewis?"

"Can you shut the door?"

She was edging back out. "I'm not supposed to be in the room alone with a patient—"

"Please." His tone was low, pleading. His features were laced with pain and worry, the green in his eyes especially deep. "I know it's weird I'm here. I'm sorry. But I can't go anywhere else."

Refusing to keep eye contact, her pulse throbbing in her throat, she said, "What's going on?"

There was a quick rap on the door. Dr. Collins stepped in. He was wearing his trademark black turtleneck, but his coat was longer than usual. With his silver bouffant, he looked like a mad scientist.

"Duke? I'm surprised to see you back." His southern accent was particularly pronounced.

Angel handed the chart to the doctor. She hoped he didn't notice her shaking hands.

The doctor slipped on a pair of black reading glasses and smiled at her, putting a hand on her shoulder and giving her a squeeze. "There's nothing filled out, darlin'.

What've you been doing?" Then Dr. Collins turned to Duke. "Let me guess: You were an idiot and didn't stay off the ankle?"

Angel was surprised he was so abrupt. It couldn't be every day a famous baseball player came into the clinic.

"Skip the lecture, Doc. Can you just take a look?"

Dr. Collins peered at Duke over the top of his reading glasses but didn't say anything. Instead, he reached out for Duke's ankle and roughly tested his movement.

"What the hell? Come on! That hurts!"

"Angel, would you get his vitals?" The doctor waited while she put on the blood pressure cuff and wrote down the results. Both Duke and Dr. Collins were watching her closely; her skin tried to crawl off her body.

"Your BP is high," the doctor said. "I'm going to take some X-rays, to be sure your ankle's not broken. There's a lot of swelling. What did you do to it this time?"

Angel, doing her best not to touch Duke, shoved a thermometer into his mouth as he started to answer. Squinting his eyes at her in annoyance, he mumbled around the stick, "I was playing ball with some kids. They got excited and tackled me."

"That wasn't very smart, now was it, son? I'll send in the X-ray technician with the portable machine."

"Remember, don't put my name on the paperwork."

"I'd be more willing to accommodate you, Mr. Lewis, if you'd paid for the last time you were here."

"It's been paid. My financial manager was here last night."

"No, your bill is still owing."

Angel didn't understand what they were talking about, but Duke visibly seethed. "I will make a call, get the money here before I leave."

"Fine." The doctor stepped toward the doorway. "The results shouldn't take long. We're not busy."

Angel, unsure of her next move, shifted awkwardly from foot to foot. Dr. Collins swung his head from her to the ballplayer and narrowed his eyes. "Come on, Nurse," he said. "There's plenty of other people for you to help." He held open the door, waiting for Angel to exit.

Sliding past him, she was relieved to not be stuck in a room with Duke. She'd never felt more awkward in her life. But that relief didn't last for long.

"Get the tech in there," Dr. Collins said to her, once they were in the hall. "As soon as he's done with X-rays, stabilize the patient's ankle. Use the compression wrap, but include a layer of the precut foam. I want it to be difficult for him to move. We might want to put a cast on him, just to be safe. That man doesn't listen." He moved down the corridor, but over his shoulder he said, "Don't be in there alone with him, Angel. I don't trust him."

Yeah. 'Cuz you're trustworthy . . .

It took the tech only a few minutes to get film on Duke's ankle. Angel muttered under her breath when the technician wheeled his machine back out of the ballplayer's room. She was not ready to go in, and there was no else around.

Leaving the door propped open, Angel went directly to the drawers, nervously opening and shutting them as she gathered materials for a soft splint. Finally, when she had everything she needed, she calmed her breathing and turned around.

He was staring at her.

"So," she stammered. "You are the Duke."

"And you are the nurse. Not a stripper."

"Ha ha. Very funny." She laid the wrap and foam next to him. "I'm supposed to wrap your ankle. You might end up with a cast anyway, even if your ankle isn't broken. Dr. Collins thinks it might be the only way to make sure you keep it immobilized."

"Oh, hell no!" the ballplayer burst out, panic tightening his face.

She took a step back. "Don't shoot the messenger."

"You don't understand. My manager or the GM sees me with a cast and I'm gonna be benched. Maybe for the season. They have me on a short leash."

"If you broke your ankle, you couldn't play anyway, could you?"

He put his head into his hands. "This can't be happening. If I can't keep up with children, how am I going to play the Red Sox?"

She tried to comfort him, saying stiffly, "I know it seems bad, but you'll be okay. It'll work out." He didn't answer. She dragged over a stool and sat in front of him. Gathering her courage, she grasped his calf and brought his foot into her lap. Without looking up or saying a word, she wrapped his ankle, first layering on the foam. Her fingertips brushed against his skin, again and again, making it impossible to forget kissing him the day before—or the mortifying rejection.

"You're very gentle, thank you."

"Of course." Applying the Ace bandage, she dared to glance up at him briefly. "I'm sorry my son and his team did this to you." *And I am so sorry I kissed you.*

She dropped her eyes back to his ankle, but Duke said, "No way was it those kids' fault. They was just playin'."

She attached the end of the wrap with the Velcro tab and then ran her hands over it to make sure it was secure. The hard muscle of his calf was distracting. "Um, I hope I didn't wrap this too high or tight."

"It's fine." He wiggled his toes, not moving his foot from her lap. "I had fun yesterday. But it was stupid of me to run around like that."

There was a knock on the door, and then a strange man's voice floated in through the half-open door. "Duke?"

"Aaron?"

The door popped all the way open. A wild-eyed man in a business suit stomped into the room. It was the driver from the park the day before. "Dude!"

"What are you doing here? How'd you find me?"

"The press."

Duke awkwardly removed his foot and tried to stand up, but almost lost his balance. "What?"

"There's a gaggle of them outside. Someone recognized you and called the paparazzi. You're already trending, man. TMZ tweeted out 'The Bronx Bolts pitcher is at a medical urgent care!' and now the internet is blowing up." He stared at Duke's wrapped ankle. "How bad?"

"I'm just faking it. I'm really here to see Angel. Stop worrying. It's nothing."

Angel froze.

"The woman who kissed you yesterday?" The agent finally noticed her trying to be invisible along the back wall. "Yeah. Duke, that is brilliant!"

"No!"

"I don't care if you're paralyzed, you need to walk out of here and make those paparazzi believe you are totally one hundred percent. The hot bartending nurse understands that, right?"

"What'd you call me? And understand *what*?"

Duke sighed. "He's saying he wants you to pretend to be my girlfriend."

"Wha—Oh. You want the reporters to think Duke came to see me."

"Right-o. She smart, Duke." Aaron rocked up and down on his two-thousand-dollar heels. "Angel, no offense, but I saw you lay one on our man here. A famous pitcher. VIP. Beloved by the people. This should be your dream come true. He's the perfect date, right?"

"Are you serious?" Her hands clenched. How dare he talk to her that way? *Besides, Duke might be the perfect date, but he is not the perfect man. How can someone so talented and wealthy be so messed up?*

"Aaron, shut up." Duke turned to Angel, stepping between the two of them. He glanced down at her closed fists and put his hand out to her. "He's a jerk. He can't help it."

His fingers were warm, wrapped around her hand. She yanked free. *I'm not about to get sucked into him again.*

Dr. Collins strode in with the X-rays just in time to see her pull away from Duke. Irritation flitted across his face. The small room grew smaller. Angel composed herself, tried to get back her professional demeanor, and began cleaning up the wrappers and extra gauze, straightening the exam room counters. *I'm all business, Dr. Collins. Nothing to see here.*

The doctor hung the films on the light box and flipped the switch. "You're not broken, Duke. See? Whole bones. Like I said, the muscles damaged by the gunshot wound are taking their time to heal completely. You can see the wound is closed and knitted back together. You simply need to let the muscles have more time to strengthen. You tweaked them good. We should put on a cast as a precaution."

"Nope. Not happening. Thanks for your time, Doctor. Let's go, Aaron." Duke turned to Angel. "Coming?"

She felt her face redden. "Are you crazy?"

He put his hand out to her again, this time palm up. "Maybe. But I need you. If you can walk outside with me, let the press take your picture, and pretend like we're going on a date, you'll be saving my career."

"No way. Besides, what's it matter if they find out now or next week that your ankle is sprained?"

Duke's voice was steel. "I will be ready for practice. End of story."

Aaron butted in. "You thought it was broken, Duke? It hurts that bad?"

Duke ignored him, focused on Angel. Her insides shivered. She needed to get control of the situation—and herself. "I don't have time for this. You're a rock star. Go make something up. They love you."

Dr. Collins surprised Angel, stepping close and slinging an arm around her shoulders. "What's going on here?"

She hunched away from his embrace as politely as she could.

The corners of Duke's mouth drew down as he folded his arms and leaned against the counter. "You guys don't get it! They're not going to politely leave because I tell them I'm okay. They're dogs with a bone; they're going to dig until they find the biggest story. They love the copy I give them, not me." He focused on Angel. "You know why I left yesterday? Aaron called to tell me reporters were on their way to the park. They stalk me twenty-four hours a day, and they always find me, waiting for me to fall down drunk or take a swing at someone."

The doctor, perplexed, said, "This doesn't seem like Angel's problem."

"I can handle this, Dr. Collins." She didn't bother hiding the irritation in her voice. To Duke, she said, "Why can't a reporter do a story about you helping out at a youth baseball practice? I'd think your bosses would like that."

"Sure, that part was fine. But if a photographer had been there when I hurt my ankle? I'd be screwed."

Aaron said, "Like right now."

"This is all well and good, but Angel is my nurse. She's not leavin' with you." The doctor's tone was possessive.

"What if I pay you for her time?" Aaron said.

"Y'all building quite the tab." The doctor's eyes narrowed. "It seems to me we should consider terms of negotiation, considering how important it is to you boys to keep these little visits quiet."

"You know this isn't 1812, right?" Angel burst out, closing her eyes in frustration, trying to dampen her temper in front of her boss—who was not only a perv but also apparently a blackmailer. Speaking in a measured tone, instead of yelling or cursing, she said, "I actually get to decide when and what I do, and I'm sure the hell not for sale." She started for the door. "I'm not getting involved in this mess. I'm out."

"Please don't go!" Duke hadn't moved, but his eyes swallowed her. "I'm not trying to be a jerk. My life is shit without baseball. I have to get back into the game. Please."

Her heart tugged at the hurt she could hear in his voice. He might be rich and famous and entitled, but there was an ache in him. However, it wasn't until she reached for the door handle that a thought struck her, stopping her feet.

This is the man who calmed Jose when he was so sick. And this guy hurt himself practicing with the boys' team. Jose would want her to help. She struggled, wanting to stay clear of drama and maintain her pride but also wanting her son to know she did the right thing.

He's asking me to be friendly and get my picture taken. It'll be over in two minutes.

She straightened her ponytail, making a decision. "Dr. Collins, it's time for me to clock out anyway. Duke, if you want to walk me outside, I suppose it won't kill me."

She ignored Aaron and the doctor as they exchanged a nod. Duke limped out after her.

Duke held her up.

He had to. Angel's slight frame went rubbery as the crush of people swarmed them, swinging microphones around, shotgunning the air with their questions. Thousands of lightning bolts burst from cameras, aimed at their faces. Her fine, fine face. Stepping out onto the sidewalk, facing the press, wearing her green scrubs and old Adidas, her hair messy and adorable, a proud, hardworking *mamita* . . . She had no idea how beautiful she was. Or what was in store for her. Reporters were going to want her story, pointing cameras in her windows and trying to get on elevators with her.

She's not like the other women I know. I shouldn't do this to her.

Angel turned her face up to his, fear boiling deep in her golden eyes. He kept his arm around her waist, letting her know she wasn't alone. He was proud of her when she bit her lip but then curved her mouth into a smile and faced the crowd.

"Duke! Duke! Who is this? Are you hurt? Why are you at a clinic? How come you're not at training camp?"

"Yo, you guys, chill out. I report next week, as planned. I'm just here to pick up this sweet thing." He grinned at the nurse fidgeting at his side.

"Is she your girlfriend? What about Regina? What's she think?"

Who gives a fuck what she thinks? "Regina is very old news."

"Honey, what's your name? Are you Duke's girl?"

Panic flashed across Angel's face. Her body swayed. He tucked her into his side, where she fit perfectly. "This is Angel. I hope you folks are gonna be nice; she's a great girl."

She tilted her face up to him, her expression innocent and irresistible. There was nothing cagey or calculating about the woman.

Without thinking, his hand spread across the small of Angel's back. Then he bent over and pressed his lips to hers, softly at first, respectful, partly for show, though partly for himself—he'd been wanting a second act to the kiss from yesterday.

Then her shapely mouth moved, responded, and his mind went blank, the buzz of the press disappeared. He pressed harder and she reacted with a passion he hadn't earned. Her lips parted and his tongue slid in, tasting her before she shut him out again. He felt her tremble. He pulled away before she could slap him.

"I was just returning the favor," he whispered into her ear.

Hundreds of flashbulbs were going off, lighting up the dingy February sky.

Chapter Eight

The black Mercedes SUV roared up to the curb. She was grateful when Duke's agent jumped out to herd her through the shouting crowd of reporters and into the backseat surrounded by tinted windows.

Duke slid in beside her and beamed. "You were great."

She offered her most withering stare in return, trying her damnedest to appear unruffled, thankful he couldn't see her galloping heart or the heat between her legs. "A heads-up would have been nice before you decided to make out with me. I might have been able to play it off better."

She could feel him on her lips.

He was quiet for a beat. "Yeah, I didn't plan it. Just seemed like a good idea at the time. Thanks for being a sport."

"You're lucky I didn't rip your throat out." *Actually, I came* close to ripping off your shirt. His mouth had lit a fire in her. The kiss at the field had been an accident with a stranger. This, however . . . It was intense. It was confusing. He'd seemed so passionate, but then drew away. Had she actually been hoping the kiss was real? Yes, she realized. But now it was obvious, it was simply a ploy.

I'm no famous model. He's not interested in someone like me.

She flinched. Reporters were knocking on the windows, shouting out questions.

I don't want to be famous. I don't want to be Regina.

"Man, can we get out of here?" Duke said.

"Yes, please, can we?" Angel badly wanted to be at home, hiding under the covers.

"On it." Aaron flicked on the blinker and spun the steering wheel at the same time, cutting off a fleet of taxis. The surrounding honking trebled. *Must be his signature move,* Angel thought, jolted against the seat. The agent angled the rearview mirror at her and asked, "Where do you live?"

"A couple blocks up from the Peacock, on Jerome Avenue. In the building above House of Beauty salon."

Aaron's cell rang. The agent nodded to her, then barked into his phone. "Yeah?"

She sat back. There were so many elephants in the roomy interior with her and Duke, she felt like she was about to be squashed. Duke clearly didn't know what to say, either, staring out his window. What could he say? Or maybe he was simply done with her and had no further need to talk to her.

Fortunately they were at her apartment within minutes, though it was time that dragged by painfully. She had her door open even before the car was stopped. Duke handed out her backpack as Aaron chattered into his phone at top volume.

"Thanks for the ride." She moved awkwardly from foot to foot. "Good luck with everything. I really do hope you get to play."

He was distracted by his agent's conversation but managed to say, "Tell Jose hi. I'll come by a practice if I can."

"Alright."

"Wait. Can I get your number? I owe you a drink at least, after everything."

She froze, surprised. "I don't think so, Duke."

He half-smiled. "Seriously? You don't want to get a drink with me?"

I'm probably the first woman to say no to him in a long while, if ever. "You don't owe me anything. Besides, my state boards are in a week. And my finals. I'm on my own homestretch. No time for anything else." She stepped back and gave a little wave. "Thanks again for being nice to Jose. Good luck with everything."

Angel turned to find the entire staff of the salon pressed against the window, ogling them. She pushed open House of Beauty's door, wanting to glance back but forcing herself to move forward instead. She heard the car drive away.

"Get out! Was that the baseball player?"

"Are you dating a Bronx Bolt? That's the craziest shit evah!"

She sighed. "We are not dating. Come on. We . . . run in different circles."

"Latisha showed us—you're all over Instagram and Twitter!"

"The kiss? Already?" She kept her face blank. "That was for show."

"Damn, bitch. Good show."

"You have no idea what kind of a whack show that is," Angel said, rolling her eyes.

"A millionaire whack show. Fancy parties and Kanye whack show."

"He's a mess, girls. I think he might be nice, but he's a mess. Jose and I don't need that. We're doing okay." She held out her arms to Jose, who'd yet to say a word, his face pressed to the glass. Praying his baseball hero was coming back, she guessed. "Right, baby?"

"I don't know. I like him." He ran up to her and hugged her midriff.

"And he liked you. He said to tell you he'd try to come back and help with practice."

"Okay." Then, his attention span reached, he said, "Hey, Mama, can I stay at Nelson's tonight?"

"On a Monday night? No. Go do your homework, chiquito. Actually, we'll go up and do homework together. Maybe you can help your mamita finish a report." Angel was behind with her class work. It was time to settle back into real life and get stuff done.

As they drove away from the student nurse's building, Aaron put his call on speaker.

"—better be telling the truth," said a scratchy voice, coming from a man who'd had his share of cigarettes and whiskey. "If that boy is still injured, we need to know, right now."

"Skip, I told you, he's fine."

"From my experience, agents are not on close terms with the truth. Don't fuck with me, son. I'm supposed to believe he just happened to be at a clinic to see a girl? We gave him a break last year, but if he can't play, he's out. That's the way it's gotta be, and you know it. And no more scandals. Period."

The phone clicked off.

"He's mad, huh?" Duke sounded calm, but bile rose in his throat. He rolled down the window and leaned back into the seat, hoping wind in his face would help the sickening panic. *What am I going to do? Who am I if I am not playing?*

"Bro, for sure the manager's got his new pitching recruit on speed dial. Straight up, Duke, are you ready for camp? It's not just *your* career on the line, you know."

"I got this. I swear."

"The GM do not believe you." Aaron paused. "We've got to get that girl back. She can't just disappear now. Or you're gonna get replaced."

Chapter Nine

Running on autopilot, Angel made dinner for Jose, read to him, and got him to bed. Then she went to her room, found thick socks and a sweater, and returned to the living room. The tiny kitchen table was covered in a jigsaw puzzle Jose had been working on, so she put together her desk—which meant turning off the heat as she placed a wooden shelf over the radiator, laid out her notes and textbooks and computer, and pulled up a rickety chair.

She almost got back up to pour herself a glass of wine. No, she thought. *Later. Stay on task. Shut out the world.* She thumbed through the stack of paper until she found the outline and list of resources she'd created for the assignment. Then she opened up her website browser.

ESPN, TMZ, *Entertainment Tonight*, and a slew of other websites were posting pictures of her and Duke mashing faces in front of the clinic.

The media speculation about Duke's health, and the hype about his new "girlfriend," were somehow news. Reporters had tried to find out more about her from the clinic staff, but no one had given them any real details. Not yet, anyway. Only that she worked at the clinic and her first name. "Isn't she an Angel?," ran the taglines. "He must be in heaven." "An Angel brings the cure." "She must have a great bedside manner." They referred to her as a nurse, a doctor, a physical therapist . . . but never a mom. At least Jose hadn't been dragged into the mess.

They also did not know that twice she had kissed Duke and twice he had been repulsed. Polite but repulsed.

Waves of embarrassment and self-loathing lapped against her. And a solid dose of anger toward Duke, for tripping her up. She stood and paced around the small living space, trying to loosen the anxiety gripping her chest. *I do not have time for this nonsense.* She rubbed her temples. *Don't think about it. My fifteen minutes are already up. I'm never going to see Duke again. Put your head down and get to work, Angel. But let's reconsider that glass of wine.*

She took a water goblet out of the dishwasher and emptied the last of a bottle of pinot into it. Back at her computer, she took a long drink and thought, *Nothing but light reading from now on.* Closing out all but one tab, she went to the Centers for Disease Control website.

Ten minutes later she was pale-faced and shaking, thoughts of Duke shoved aside for the night. When she'd chosen the effects of asthma on children as her thesis, Angel thought she'd be killing two birds with one stone: getting a grade while also learning more about Jose's condition. But the topic choice didn't just kill birds—it almost killed her, via a massive spike in blood pressure. *Because, hey, guess what, according to the CDC, black children are twice as likely as white kids to have asthma, but ten times more likely to die from asthma complications. Ten. Times.* She'd been giving Jose albuterol, to which, apparently, black and Puerto Rican kids had the highest rate of bad responses—*including dying*. Advair was even worse, with an eightfold risk of death. But there were no alternatives.

Jose was both Puerto Rican and African American. The kid couldn't catch a break.

She went to bed hours later, her eyes red and aching from staring at a computer screen. And from drinking. But, really, from crying.

Duke shuddered awake when his phone rang, yanking him from a deep, troubled sleep. *Skip calling back, deciding to make a clean break.*

He groped for the phone and tried to read the sleep-blurred screen. It was Roland.

"Man, why are you calling this early?"

"Hi, this is Kinley," said a woman with a posh accent. "And it's eight o'clock in the morning. Get up, for God's sakes."

"Oh, Kinley, hi. I was expecting your old man."

"I stole his phone," she said. "So, who's the girl, Duke? Roland says she's a stripper?"

Kinley had always been good to Duke, probably a better friend than Roland. After Mark was shot, she'd called a number of times, to check in, and had sent groceries while he healed. When Regina left him, Kinley came to his house, trying to talk him out of his funk, and had even tactfully suggested rehab if he was going to keep self-medicating. She was friends with Regina, but Kinley made it clear she didn't like how the model had treated Duke when the guy was down.

He rolled onto his back, flopping an arm over his eyes to block out the morning light. "Tell Roland to shut the hell up. She is not a stripper and he knows it."

"I assumed he was full of it. Just wanted to be sure."

"She's a nurse. Well, almost. And she's nice, Kinley." *Different than any woman I know.*

"Invite her to our party tonight. I'd like to meet her."

He paused. How much should he tell Kinley? He didn't want to lie to his friends but, on the other hand, it was clear he was going to have to talk Angel into going out with him a few more times, anyway, until the clubhouse calmed down.

"Huh. I'd like to, but she's, uh, maybe not set for your kind of party, Kinley."

She laughed. "I'm not judgy-judgy like that, and you

know it. But I wouldn't want the poor girl to feel out of place. Do you have her address? I can send her a dress and shoes. She looks about my size, unless the cameras added ten pounds." She laughed again. "Is she a good kisser?"

"I'm a gentleman. Never kiss and tell, I say."

She sniffed, ladylike. "Right."

He lay in bed after hanging up, trying to create a plan of attack. Kinley and Roland had offered a solution. Plenty of people would see Angel and Duke together if they went to this fancy cocktail party. But he wasn't sure how he felt about disrupting the student nurse's life again, much less how he would talk her into it. She'd been adamant about getting back to her regular life. Something about exams? He caught a glimpse of himself in the mirror on the wall across the room. If he was being fair, he really should leave the poor woman alone. She deserved better.

A few minutes later, his phone beeped. Kinley had taken the planning out of his hands.

Her text said Aaron was delivering an invitation, dress, and shoes to Angel's building, and that Duke was to pick her up that evening, flowers in hand.

Duke sighed. Kinley hadn't wasted any time.

He and Angel had never exchanged phone numbers, so she had no way of saying no until he went to pick her up. *Is it right to do this to her?* He could only hope she'd be swayed by the invitation and Kinley's present. There was a fifty-fifty shot he'd show up and Angel would be wearing yoga pants and slam the door in his face. *I bet she looks cute in yoga pants, though.*

Angel stood over Jose. He smiled in his sleep as early-morning sun streamed through the grimy window. The boy's small chest rose and fell rhythmically under the quilt his *abuela* had made for him, each knot imbued with the deep love of a grandma. Angel wanted to climb under the blanket, cuddle up to her son's warmth and his innocence, and sleep for a week.

He was so peaceful, not a care in his little world. She bent over and kissed his forehead lightly, blanketing him with more love, pouring prayers of protection onto him. Because spring, with its pollen and molds, was on the way. Death was on the horizon. A tear rolled down her nose and dropped onto his forehead.

No more of that. It's not the zombie apocalypse. Get ahold of yourself.

Fifteen minutes later, a sleepy Jose shared an apple, egg, and toast with Angel while she watched CNN. When she asked Jose if he knew where his shoes were, she heard a reporter say Duke's name. And hers.

A national network was playing a video clip of the green-eyed Bronx Bolt pitcher holding a startled woman in scrubs. It was like a scene out of *Gone with the Wind* as he locked his lips onto hers. She saw herself shut her eyes and respond enthusiastically. His expression was intense, passionate. It made for good TV.

"Mama?"

"Yes, I know. That's me."

"You *are* hooking up with the Duke!"

"I am not hooking up with anybody. He was giving me a thank-you kiss, for helping him with something. Like the other day."

The announcer said, *"It looks like the Duke's heart has been mended after what was undeniably a rough year for the seasoned pitcher. Hopefully, a smooch from his new girlfriend bodes well for the season. Good luck, Duke!"*

Jose grinned at her, now wide awake. She could only imagine the excited gossip among the kids in his classroom that day.

As he finished tying his shoes, she changed out of scrubs, into jeans and a T-shirt, put on a peacoat with a high collar, and tugged a beanie down over her hair. Catching a glimpse of herself in a mirror, she felt like an actor in a movie. She was a student nurse; who was she to be going incognito?

She walked Jose to school, then hopped the bus to Bronx Community College, arriving just as her morning lecture started. She quietly slid into a back row and kept her hat on, not making eye contact with anyone. After an hour of scribbling notes and realizing exactly how far behind she was and how much she didn't know, she headed outside with the rest of the class.

"Angel, I saw you on the—"

She spun around to cut off Theresa, who was bouncing along excitedly behind her. "Shh! I don't want anyone to know. As a matter of fact, I don't want to talk about it. It was a weird, onetime thing."

The other nursing student shrugged good-naturedly. "Fine. I'd be a little more excited about it, but whatever. Do you want to meet with the study group at Rue la Rue's Café?" Her eyes were wide and expectant, though Angel had not attended one study session with the group. Always working or with Jose.

"I can't today, but thank you for asking." She was relieved that Theresa didn't press her about Duke.

Angel returned a wave as the other student sauntered away. Then she suddenly flushed with a rush of jealousy so strong she almost went to her knees. The study group was a bunch of normal twenty-year-old college students, able to spend the day in a café and update their social media while scarfing down pizza and quizzing each other on Latin terms, and then stay up until two in the morning playing beer pong and hooking up with Tinder dates.

Angel took the bus back home. She *was* going to study, but she also had to take care of family errands. She had one stop to make first.

The Peacock was closed in the morning, but there were cars in the parking lot, including Frank's orange Viper. *Time to pull up my big girl panties.* The front doors were unlocked. Entering the bar in the daytime was always such an odd experience. The air was clear. The natural light coming in through high windows revealed beautiful marble tables and cedar-paneled walls that, in the candlelight and bar lights, looked totally different.

She waited by the bar for a minute, absorbing the sounds. She didn't hear any sex screams, only the ice machine cranking out rocks and the heaters warming up the cement floors.

Voices came from the kitchen in the back. Pushing through swinging doors, she walked into a wide-open room with smoking grills and delicious smells. The famous farm-to-table chef, a James Beard Award winner from Portland, refused to talk to any of the help but knew the animals he cooked by name. Angel could see him hand-grinding spices while barking at three or four minions who were massaging kale and caressing lamb shanks. At a side table sat the club owner, sampling an array of dishes.

Frank lifted something black and slimy. "You should try this, it's great. No, wait. What are you doing here? I fired you."

"I need my job back."

"You attacked a Bronx Bolt! And he's a homey, no less! Of all the famous people who come in here, you go after a beloved Bronxite? You couldn't throw something at Tom Cruise?"

"I can if you want me to."

"You know what, Angel, I can joke. You can't. Your problem is, you don't know your place."

"Frank." She swallowed, hard. "I am sorry. If you are willing to let me come back, I'll be a model employee."

"I don't know. The staff don't like you. You snap at people. You're bitchy."

Angel bit her lip. It was true, she did snap at the workers—they were slow and lazy. "What if I promise to be sweet as pie?"

"I'd like to see that."

Let it go.

Then he offered a grin that instantly made her suspicious. "If you promise you can get the Duke to come back in, you're on. I saw the kiss. He must like getting drinks thrown on him. I wonder if he's one of those guys who likes golden showers."

"Why you always gotta go there, Frank?" She rolled her eyes. "Yes, I'll get him to come back in." *Not in a million years.* "Can I work tonight?"

"Can you get him to come in here tonight?"

She stammered. "No, no, not tonight." *Even if I wanted to ask him this favor, I don't have his number.*

"Then, no. Like I said, get him to come back, maybe even have his picture taken by the marquee, and we'll talk."

"Fine."

She stomped back out into the daylight. *No way am I asking Duke that. I am not asking anyone for anything. I'll be damned if I have to lower myself again. I'll clean hotels until I get a nursing job.*

A few minutes later, trudging up the narrow stairs to

her apartment, she calculated how many hours she had free to study. Jose would be home from school around three. In the meantime, she could take a practice test, review two or three medical articles, and vacuum up the daily layer of dust provided by the number 4 train. She tried to remember what was in her cupboard. She was pretty sure she had enough ingredients for *sopa de pollo con mofongo*, the traditional soup her mama had made. She'd have to substitute canned ham for the chicken, and a bag of frozen vegetables for the fresh carrots and peas and celery, but Angel had plantains and couple strips of bacon left—she could make the *mofongo* balls she and Jose both loved. It would not be nearly as good as her mama's, but comfort food was comfort food.

She flashed again on Theresa and the study group, having midday cocktails and tapas, free to do nothing but study or swipe left on their iPhones.

Angel didn't have an iPhone. She didn't do Tinder. Or dates. She wasn't free to have drinks in the middle of the day. She wasn't a kid. She hadn't been a kid since the day Jose was born. At fifteen, she'd created something, and, accidentally or not, she was responsible. She only stayed up until two in the morning if she was studying or Jose was throwing up. She was a mother. She'd turned her back on her childhood and free time and walked away.

She didn't have time to resent it.

Leaning against her door was a large package.

"Ahem," said a voice behind her.

She jumped a foot and whirled around. She grimaced when she realized it was Aaron, Duke's agent. "What are you doing here?"

He handed her an envelope and gestured to the box. "Duke sent this over."

Chapter Ten

"Gabriela!" Angel shouted, bursting into the salon with the long box.

A half-dozen women swiveled toward her.

"What? What's wrong?"

"The Duke sent me this!"

Gabriela frowned at her. "Good Lord. Unless that is a human head, stop your screeching. You just gave me a stroke."

"What'd that fine man send you?" Latisha called from her station.

Angel placed the box on the floor in front of her, removed a piece of thick, creamy paper, and handed it to Gabriela. "Duke wants me go to a cocktail party with him tonight . . ."

It took all her strength to not complete that sentence,

that the Duke and his agent *needed* her to go to the party. As his beard, to keep up the charade for his manager.

She'd told Aaron she'd think about going, and then left him standing in the hall as she went into her apartment and shut the door, not wanting to give him the chance to steamroll her with a sales pitch. But she just couldn't see how it was a good idea. It would not be responsible or prudent for her to take up so much time doing something so pointless and frivolous. Pointless for her, anyway.

Gabriela read the note. "Oh my God. It's at Roland and Kinley Smith's Park Avenue penthouse."

"Isn't she the reality TV star? I love her," said a customer dressed from shoe to choker in leopard print, her eyes wide beneath a head of hot rollers.

"What do I do? I can't go."

"Why in the hell not?"

"This is crazy. I've got Jose, and work, and tests coming up." *And I don't want to be anyone's fake girlfriend.* It was embarrassing enough to be on the news; what would happen when the media figured out it was a ruse?

"You trippin'. If it's 'cuz you need something to wear, we got you covered. Right, girls?"

Angel cut through a round of excited offers. "No! That's not it." She bent over the box, tugged sheets of tissue free, and then slowly withdrew a red cocktail dress with a low back and crisscrossed material covering the breasts.

"Oh. My. God. Is that a *Balmain*?" Gabriela's eyes bugged out. Her addiction to fashion magazines was evident.

"Yes. How do I send it back?"

"You are joking, right?"

"I would stick out like a sore thumb at this party. A freaking country mouse. There will be movie stars and rock stars. Kinley's family's business is listed in the Fortune Five Hundred. Can you see me standing in a living room, chatting it up with a hedge fund manager? Or Jay-Z? Wearing this ridiculous dress?"

"Yes!" six women yelled at once.

"No, no, no. I have got to study. I can't go running off to parties in the middle of the week."

"You don't go to parties on the weekends. Or ever."

"How do I find his address? His phone number? I need to tell him no and send this back," she said stubbornly. But her hand caressed the material of the dress. So soft. So fine.

"Honey, even if I knew how to find that information, I wouldn't help you. Take that stick out of your ass. You will not be struck down by lightning if, for once in your life, you give yourself a night off. And what a fucking night, woman!"

Latisha jumped in. "She being nice. Let me tell you what the rest of us are thinking: No one needs to go out and party more than you. You the tightest-wound bitch I know."

"No! You guys don't understand! He doesn't even like me!" She stopped. She had to be careful with what she said. She'd promised not to say anything that could get Duke in trouble. But he was pushing this too far.

"You was fine leavin' Jose with me if you was wor-kin'," Gabriela said. "And every man who walks past you pants like a dog. Of course the Duke wants you. He kissed you! Don't play dumb." She took the dress and held it up to Angel. "Do you have shoes?"

"There's a pair in the box."

The box was practically ripped apart. The women fell back with a collective sigh as Latisha held up a pair of spike heels with onyx straps.

"I think . . . I think those are Tom Fords," said one woman in a hushed whisper, her eyes glazed over.

Latisha dug out her phone, took a picture, and dropped the photo into Google Images. The results were imme-diate. "No. Those are Zanottis. The pair Kim Kardashian wore to a fund-raiser in Paris a few months ago. How much is twelve hundred lira?"

"Don't you mean francs?"

"How often am I in France, bitch?"

"Actually, I think they use the euro."

"Okay, euros . . . Jesus. Those shoes are thirteen hun-dred U.S. dollars."

"What about the dress?"

"Umm. Okay, Angel, don't freak out. It's four thousand. Not available in stores yet."

Gabriela quickly walked over to the window and hung the dress on the curtain rod. The women were afraid to touch it. Angel's heart was skipping beats. "I—"

"Stop right there. Before you argue any more, try it on. Let's at least see what it looks like." Gabriela held up a hand. "I'm guessing you don't have a pair of Spanx. I will be right back." She darted out the door.

"What about a bra?" Angel called after her, eying the backless dress.

Latisha snorted. "Honey. The designer is a genius. Those crossed strips plump up your titties and cover what needs to be covered. Show the man some skin and maybe he will climb on board."

"Ugh. I don't want him on board! I'm certainly not wearing Spanx and going braless to please a man."

"Girl, you don't ever do nothin' to please a man. Usually, I say, 'Great. You do you.' But come on, give just a little. Give in to the thirst."

"Look, Angel." One of the quieter stylists, who did makeup for wedding parties and was always on point, held out an iPad. "This is the palette and makeup map for your skin color and face shape. I'd love to help with your makeup. Will you let me?"

Gabriela reappeared, dropped the black shapewear into her chair, and clapped her hands. "Hell yes, girls. A makeover!"

Angel tried to wave away the instant buzz in the room, everyone jumping up and down like teenagers at the thought of a makeover. "I have not said I'm going!" she yelled.

Latisha jabbed a straightener at her. "I've heard a lot of whiny baby-bitching coming from you. But not an actual no."

"What? You are high *and* deaf."

"Maybe. But whatever was comin' out of your mouth was not comin' from your heart. Or you wouldn't have hauled ass down here in the first place, with your dress and your shoes and your invitation to the ball. So you need help with your hair."

"Is that a question?"

"No."

Angel knew she had a point. That, in her heart, she did want to go. The consequence would probably be humiliation when the world found out the truth, but, on the other hand, they would be more focused on Duke than on her. She'd fade back into the background quickly enough. But first, she'd get to dress in haute couture and see some of the most famous people in New York, hopefully from a quiet corner. She could take one night off from reality. She would never have this opportunity again.

Gabriela saw her face soften, and let out a whoop. The salon owner quickly marshaled the troops, before Angel could change her mind. They each had assigned tasks, everyone responsible for at least one body part. The room full of women eagerly threw themselves into Project Angel, morphing into a finely honed glamour squad.

By the time Angel showered and returned to the shop, having followed very specific body grooming instructions, the ladies had set up the salon like a surgical theater, with hair, makeup, and nail supplies at the ready. *Thank God there isn't time for a full body wax.* Gabriela had warned her before she went upstairs: "I'm gonna check. If you don't take care of that bush, we are going to hold you down and wax you bald."

"Jesus, you don't need to be so up in my business." But shave she did—legs, armpits, bikini area. *As if anyone is going to be seeing Miss Thing tonight.*

She knew exactly why she was being asked to the press-heavy party, but sitting in Gabriela's chair, up high like she was on the Iron Throne, wearing a cardigan over the shapewear, surrounded by ladies amped to hummingbird level, she started to get excited. While Duke maybe wasn't into her, he was nice. And, well, damn, the *Balmain*. The luscious, deep red satin glowed in the window where the dress hung, sharp AF.

"You're not doing anything crazy to me, like turquoise-and-yellow blocked eye shadow or snogged lips. I want blending and I want lip liner. I want classic, nothing that's going to make me stand out."

"Oh, we goin' make you stand out. In all the right ways. From motherfucking fleek eyebrows to the perfect J. Lo glow."

Angel sat quietly, living in the moment for the first time in a very long time. *I might as well give in to it, enjoy the ride.*

The makeup artist brought in a suitcase of beauty

supplies. One large container was home to at least twenty brushes.

"Seriously, how many makeup brushes do you need?"

"They different sizes. Some are firm, some soft. They're for contouring." The girl put the iPad in Angel's lap and tapped the striped face on the screen. "Each of those layers is a different foundation or powder, either highlighting, covering, or downplaying certain features. These brushes are for shading or for blending."

"Painting my face for real. Nice." Angel owned one brush for the one shade of blush she'd worn for years—when she wore anything.

"The Prada makeup artist says we use face paint as a statement and as a form of self-expression," the girl said. "Not to please other people."

Angel liked that. It soothed away at least one angst niggling at her, the worry that she was stepping on her feminist principles if she was too girly. *Feminism is about being free to be myself*, she thought, *and this is who I want to be tonight. A princess. No, a queen. Just for night.*

Her face changed over the next couple of hours. She didn't become someone different; the artist brought out her unique features, highlighting the beauty she hadn't realized was there. Angel was awed by the smoky black cat eye. It made her look sexy and fierce. She decided to wake up every day and immediately outline her eyes with a thick Marilyn Monroe wing. She felt strong and beautiful, admiring the black gel liner and shadow, a gold shimmer lightly layered over the black on the lid and along the lower lashes.

Her eyebrows were shaped to suit her pixie face. Fake eyelashes were attached in the middle and allowed to flutter at the ends. As a final touch, the artist used a silver holographic glitter on the inside corner of the eyes and along the outer edge of the shadow, and then dusted it along the top of Angel's high cheekbones as a highlighter.

"You gorgeous!" Gabriela said, hands on her hips, face lit up with happiness for Angel. "Your face is beat!"

"You should work for M.A.C.," Angel told the artist. The young woman had magic in her.

Two of the salon ladies had been working on her nails, one at each hand. They'd applied acrylics, shaped the nails perfectly, and painted on a rich gold color. Angel loved it. *It looks like I dipped my fingers in liquid gold, it's so pretty.*

Through it all, Gabriela slaved over Angel's dark mass of long, spiraling curls, clapping back at the unwanted advice and jabs from the roomful of stylists. When Angel had first sat in Gabriela's chair, her friend had undone her ponytail and run her hands through Angel's hair, gently detangling it and fluffing it out. "Look at you, girl. This hair is amazing. I can't believe you stick it in a ponytail every day."

"Mama used to run her fingers through my hair like that," Angel said dreamily. She hadn't meant to say it aloud. Gabriela caught her eye in the mirror and nodded sympathetically. Angel pictured her mama sitting next to her on the stoop on a sunny summer morning, folding her long, wild hair into braids. Tears welled in her eyes.

Latisha saved her, pressing tissues to the corners of her eyes. "Stop being a pussy. You're going to smear your makeup." Her cutting remarks weren't real, though; she patted Angel's shoulder before walking away to retrieve hair product.

In the end, Gabriela and Angel agreed on an edgy chignon-like bun, but with more lift. A colored rinse, drying the roots, flat iron, roller set, brush out, a doobie with pin curls, finger combing, and looping the smooth, volumized hair into a bun . . . As a last step, the baby hairs left around her face were waxed and softened.

"Respect, girl. You look like J. Lo at the Oscars," Latisha said. "Maybe even prettier." The women clustered in a semicircle around her, nodding.

"I'm afraid to put on the dress."

Chapter Eleven

Duke could hear his father on the phone as he made his way down the long staircase. He couldn't hear exactly what he was saying but it sounded like a hushed argument. His ears perked up; he swore he heard his father say Regina's name. *Why?*

Willis hung up as Duke entered the kitchen. "Hey, Pops, who you talking to?"

"About time you got your lazy ass out of bed."

Duke would have laughed. But his father wasn't joking. "Pops, are you for real? Who bought this house?"

"You are damn lucky you playin' ball, boy. What else would you do? They don't pay young men to sit around and play video games."

"Why you ridin' me?"

"You upstairs sleepin' when you should be out running

or lifting weights. You're going to be sloppy next week. Fat and slow. Get your act together, Duke. If you want to be a success, you have to act like it."

"I *am* a success. Who do you think you're talking to?"

"I'm talking to a brother who's close to washing out."

"Have I ever been good enough for you?"

"That is a ridiculous, self-pitying question. I simply want you to be better. How much money do you think you'll make in the minors?"

"This is about money, then."

"Son, I'd like to say you are set up for the rest of your life. But you're not."

Duke growled in anger at his father. "Why are my credit cards canceled? You stealin' my money?"

"Damn it, boy. I have busted my ass, sweating it out late at night while you were off renting yachts and buying cases of Moët, feeling sorry for yourself—and I was paying off the lawyers. I was worried you were going to prison. Believe you me, that was a chunk of change. We are still paying for that. More than you know."

"You thought I was going to prison? You thought I was guilty?" Duke's face contorted. "Of what? Did you think I killed Mark?"

His father blustered and waved his hands. "I knew, whatever the truth was, you are a black man and your chances of having something pinned on you were fairly high."

"Come on! 'Whatever the truth'? Thanks, Pops. Thanks

a lot. You always know what to say to make me feel warm and cuddly." He paused. "Why didn't you tell me how much money we were burning through?"

"Duke, there is nothing here for you to worry about. Your new contract kicks in soon. Just go play ball. We'll get on top again."

"Oh, we will, will we?" Duke almost kicked the couch, remembering his ankle just in time. "You're telling me I'm worthless and I better work harder and make more, while you jack around with the money."

"If you think you can do this without me, fine, I'm done helping."

His ability to dance around the truth continued to amaze Duke. "Let me make it easy for you. You're fired."

A vein throbbed in Willis's neck. "You are making a big mistake."

Duke walked out.

"You look like a movie star, Mama." Jose spoke in a hushed whisper, peering at her shyly from behind Gabriela.

Her reflection in the mirror was shocking. She poked the glass. *No, it's me alright.*

She did look like a movie star, her eyes sparkling, her skin glowing, her hair smooth and perfect. The dainty high heels elongated her legs, showing off heart-shaped calf muscles earned from running up and down the clinic halls or standing for hours behind the bar. The red dress glimmered and emphasized her curves and Spanx-flattened stomach, lifting and covering her breasts just enough to be sexy without being scandalous.

"How can I thank you, Gabriela? Latisha? All of you! I can't believe it!"

"You can thank us by taking selfies with every hot, rich guy you meet. And then getting their number."

Jose rounded on the stylist. "Auntie Latisha, that would be rude. You would never do that to the Duke, would you, Mama?" His face was pinched with concern.

"Honey, this isn't a real date. You know that, right? We're just going as . . . friends."

"He's kissed you. He likes you. Don't you like him?"

"He doesn't like me, Jose, not like you think."

"I don't kiss my friends that are girls like that."

The ladies in the room erupted in laughter. Jose grumbled, "Not funny," and stomped into the corner with the toys, turning his back on the women.

Gabriela grabbed Angel's hand, pulled her to the side, and put her hands on her shoulders. Speaking quietly while the other women returned to work, her friend said, "He does have a point, Angel. What exactly is going on with you two?"

"Can I tell you something? Promise not to say a word."

Gabriela cocked her head to the side. "Always."

"Duke and his agent asked me to pretend to be dating him."

"Why on earth—"

"The press showed up at the clinic yesterday, following Duke. He was there because he's reinjured his ankle, the one that was shot last year. He's supposed to be reporting to camp in a few days and he's hoping to be recovered by then. He doesn't want them to have a reason to bench him. So he's asked me to pretend he was at the clinic to see me."

"That is just crazy."

"Do you see now why I didn't want to go in the first place? I don't have time for a real boyfriend, much less a fake one with a whole trainload of baggage. And what happens if the press finds out I'm not really dating him? I'd be mortified."

"Yet, Jose is right," Gabriela said. "I saw the kiss he planted on you. I saw his face. He was enjoying himself. And you said you loved getting to know him at the park, back when you thought he was just a normal guy. He's still that guy."

"He's not, though. He's famous, he's rich, and he's a world-class athlete. I deal with people like him at the Peacock every day. Charming, until they don't get their way. And they don't see me as an equal. I'm a servant, as far as they are concerned. I will not put up with that shit."

"Come on. I know I only talked to him for a second, but he doesn't seem like that. I mean, he didn't grow up spending his summer in the Hamptons—he's from the Bronx. He knows the score."

"He might be from the same streets, but he's been treated like a prince since the day someone handed him a ball and realized he could throw. You grow up being told you're special, there's no way you don't have some serious narcissistic qualities."

"Okay, let's say all of this is true. That Duke can be a pretentious asshole. Why do you care? Just go tonight and have fun. Use him like he's using you." She straightened a strap. "Look at you. You look like a million bucks, like you should be wearing a tiara. All those girls are going to be jealous, so ignore their shade. Throw your own. Duke picked you, even if you're not really dating. Obviously he sees something in you."

Angel made a kissy face. "Dah-link, will you bring me another glass of Dom?" She smiled at Gabriela. If she let herself, she could have fun, pretending to be rich for just one night.

"Cute. I'm going to give you something better. Maya Angelou."

"The poet? What are you talking about?"

"Come on, girl. You seen this for years." Gabriela tapped the framed poster on the wall beside her station.

Angel had stopped noticing the picture of the female poet long ago, as well as her poem "Phenomenal Woman," the stanzas laid out in cursive. But she instantly understood what Gabriela was getting at. She'd read the lines hundreds of times, about a woman exuding strength and sensuality, and about how that confidence is what creates beauty, and power, and makes "the fellows stand or / fall down on their knees."

She stood up straight. She controlled how people perceived her. How she perceived herself.

"That's right," Gabriela nodded. "You phenomenal. Be phenomenal. But I do have something else for you." She went to a closet and returned with a white fur stole and a small jewelry box. "The wrap is from a client. When you walk in there, head high, you show them you the queen. You nobody's bitch."

Angel draped herself in the softness.

"But this . . ." Her friend opened the box. "This is from my grandmother." Inside, nestled in velvet, was a thin gold-and-diamond bracelet. "This is so you keep it real, keep it classy."

"Gabriela, are you sure?"

"Honey, with every bit of my heart I want you to wear this tonight. Just be careful with it." She tapped Angel's heart. "More importantly, be careful with this. Don't let yourself get hurt, Angel."

That is not going to happen. I know exactly who I am and who he is.

The bracelet glittered against the red of her dress and picked up the gold color on her nails, the golden glow on her skin, in her hair. "I feel so put together."

"There's a first for everything. What time is Duke supposed to get here?"

"In about ten minutes." The butterflies in her stomach must have had babies. There was a lot of action in there.

Chapter Twelve

He stopped on the sidewalk and gaped at the gorgeous woman standing on the other side of the plate glass window. The young student nurse was definitely not wearing yoga pants. He watched Angel slide her fingertips across the red satin of her dress, along her side, and then gracefully move her hand through the air, gesturing to her friends, reminding Duke of a geisha. Sensual and confident. *Damn, the girl is fine.*

Angel's plump lips broke into a smile, her eyes sparkling, laughing at something Gabriela said, and Duke felt his own face smile. In the form-fitting dress, her body bangin', she was ready to walk out on stage somewhere, an exquisite woman who deserved to be surrounded by adoring fans. *But I think she'd hate that. This one is something special, even if she does think I'm a moron,* he thought, and he pushed open the door to the salon.

• • •

"Duke!" Jose shouted, and sprinted out of his corner, past Angel and the ladies.

There in the doorway of House of Beauty, holding two dozen white roses, stood Duke, stunning in a fitted gray suit. *Valentino maybe?* she thought. *I have no idea, but he looks edible.*

"Hey, little man," Duke said, tossing a smile at Angel before drawing something from his pocket. "I have something for you."

"Whoa," Jose said, wide-eyed.

"They're tickets for the first home game." Duke squatted in front of the boy. "Seats are right behind the dugout. Thought you might like that." He stood up, smooth and sexy, wearing his suit as comfortably as sweats. "If it's okay with your mom, of course."

"Oh, she hates baseball," Gabriela cut in, winking at Jose. "But I'll take him."

"I don't hate baseball," Angel protested. "I'm just . . . not really into sports." She smiled at Duke. "I think I can make an exception this one time."

He handed the roses to Jose. "Can you hold on to these for your mama?" Then the ballplayer politely took Angel's hand. "Thank you. I know I'm asking a lot. But it'll be fun, I promise." He stepped back and swept over her with his gaze. "Girl, you look bomb in that dress! Amazing!"

He surprised her by twirling her around, a gently guided dance move. She gasped and then laughed, satin floating and feminine against her legs. He put a hand on her waist to steady her at the end of the spin, but then quickly gave her space, offering a small bow. The women in the room sighed.

"*The swing in my waist, / and the joy in my step*" . . . *I'll let myself be a phenomenal woman, and have a phenomenal night. Save reality for tomorrow.*

Chapter Thirteen

The private elevator, with teak wall panels and a small chandelier, was silent, and it climbed sixty floors to the penthouse far too quickly. As the doors slid open, Angel thought for a second she was being punked, that Duke had delivered her to a movie set. The entry hall was marble and walnut and gold, with a sweeping marble staircase too beautiful to be real. Stepping tentatively off the elevator, she could see one double doorway leading into an old-fashioned English library.

"May I take your coat, miss?" said a butler. *A butler . . . So those guys are real. Not just on Downton Abbey.*

Another set of double doors was open to reveal an immense living area jammed with well-dressed bodies. The room, layered in deep, warm colors, boasted large windows and a massive marble fireplace. Burgundy cloth covered the walls, dampening the loud voices and the instrumental blues band in a corner next to a bar.

She hadn't known what to expect, but a manly man like Roland Smith living in such a tasteful, Victorian-styled home was a surprise. The decadent Persian rugs, heavy drapes, crown moldings, carved furniture . . . This had to be Kinley. While she became famous for being a reality TV star, she was from old money. She'd built a home from deep pockets and infinite taste.

Angel tried to regroup. *This is not just about money. I am outclassed. Way outclassed.* She'd spent too much time in Gabriela's salon, looking at fashion magazines and gossip rags. She recognized the faces and the designer clothes filling the room.

With a hand at her elbow, Duke led her into the fray. He was not walking with any sign of a limp, but his pace was slow and controlled. She, on the other hand, suddenly felt gangly and awkward, clumping along like an oaf, while the women and men cluttering the floor oozed sophistication, comfortable in their skin, in their wealth, in their moneyed cliques. Women, with smooth, long hair and perfectly shaped bodies poured into Armani and Versace and Cavalli, flicked glances toward Duke and smiled, their eyes gliding right over Angel. She wasn't there.

"You came!"

Kinley Smith placed herself in front of Angel, her tawny beige skin flawless against a blue strapless Elie Saab haute couture dress, set off by an amazing diamond-and-sapphire harness, diamond hoop earrings, and silver Giuseppe Zanotti heels. Angel blinked in surprise. *She's so beautiful, I can barely look at her.*

Towering behind the smiling hostess was Roland, the recently retired Bronx Bolt, complementing his wife in his shiny navy Prada suit. He clapped Duke on the shoulder. "'Bout time you showed up."

"I'm so pleased to meet you!" Kinley grasped Angel's arms and gave her a squeeze, which rendered Angel mute. "You're an absolute doll. What would you like to drink? Roland, would you grab us a couple of glasses of champagne? That's a good place to start. Angel . . . Is that right? Angel? Oh my God, I love that name."

"Come on, babe, give the girl some room." Roland put his arm around his wife's shoulders and reached out a hand to Angel. "Nice to meet you."

Angel shook the hand of the famous Bronx Bolt first baseman. "Hi," she said weakly. *I can't believe I'm hanging out with people I've seen on TV. Not just serving them drinks. And . . . ohh M G, isn't that the guy from Everybody Hates Chris?*

"Kinley," said Duke, hugging the reality show star. "Thanks for the invite. Haven't seen you in a while."

"Roland doesn't want to go out anymore. He's getting lazy in his retirement."

"Whoa, speak for yourself. Yo' man got game, whether he on the field or not." Roland cupped her ass. "I was rockin' your world this morning, if I remember correctly."

"Classy, baby, very classy." Kinley sucked her teeth at

him. "Why are you still standing here? Champagne, remember?"

"Duke, why don't you come with me. Despite what my
wife thinks, I only have two hands."

Duke stepped away, and instantly Angel felt a void
where his body heat and physical strength had been. She
was being abandoned. She automatically fidgeted with her
dress, afraid there was going to be wardrobe malfunction
with the strappy chest, or that the top of the Spanx was
visible, or, worse, that a muffin top had sprung free.

Kinley gently took one of her hands, stilling her anxiety, and said, "Go on. I'll take Angel around and introduce
her. She'll be fine." Her words were directed to Duke, but
she was smiling at Angel.

Duke raised an eyebrow at her. Angel nodded an okay.
What else could she do? She was not about to beg him to
stay—she would not come off as weak or helpless. For
damn sure she would not let these people think they had
any power over her. She kept her back straight, head up,
and put a wall around her emotions as she followed Kinley. Angel added a purposeful swish of her hips to her
stride. *Phenomenal woman, / that's me.*

"I'm so glad you decided to come. Here, let me introduce you to some of my friends." The hostess waved at a
group of women clustered around a settee, some sitting,
some leaning, some standing, all drinking and speaking
at a hundred miles an hour. "Girls, this is Duke's . . . date?
Girlfriend? I'm sorry, sweetie, I don't really know . . ."

Angel flushed red, stammering, "Um, I, I'm just here on a date. To be honest, I don't know him that well." *Should I have said that?*

Someone said, "Mm-hm. That kiss looked like it was a baby maker. You might want to speed up the introductions."

There was a burst of laughter, but it was good-natured. Kinley went around the circle, saying the names of six or seven women. Angel didn't catch a single one, just smiled and nodded. Her fingers itched to fidget with the dress straps, but she settled for slowly twisting Gabriela's bracelet back and forth.

"Like I said, these are my closest friends. We met during long days in clubhouses. We help each other out when our men are on the road or we're managing their careers while trying to have our own lives. Believe me, if anything is going to bond a group of ladies, it's making sure you don't get shoved too far out of the spotlight."

So this is the Wives Association, then. The women beside the famous athletes.

"Ain't that the truth! Girl, if you gonna hang with the big dogs, you gotta get you a thick fur coat. I recommend chinchilla." More laughter. "Seriously, Duke seems like a real nice guy, but unless you live under a rock, you saw all his troubles aired on the TV last year. Be ready for no privacy."

Angel caught Duke's eye as he and Roland were standing by the bar, next to a quarterback she remembered from

Hanes commercials. Then she spotted Serena Williams and her jaw almost dropped. *Don't get all fangirl.*

"Oh, and every woman wants your man," said one of the wives at her side. "That is the truth. I've been in the elevator with Jerrod when a couple of young thangs handed him their panties and a room number. I was standing right there! Those bitches probably won't pull that stunt again, not unless they like being snatched bald, but that shit happens all the time."

Another woman said, "We've had a crazy chick calling our house for the last four nights. Security is trying to figure out how to stop it, but I've had to turn off the landline. Who wants to wake up to a girl fingerbangin' herself and telling my husband about it?"

"Seriously?" Kinley said.

"You know it's true."

"No, I meant you saying 'fingerbanging.' That's just gross."

"Kinley, let's get a few drinks in you, then we'll see who's got the worse mouth."

A woman with fine Eurasian features leaned in and waited for the others to get closer before saying in a low, conspiratorial voice, "I've got an appointment with a private detective tomorrow. Nicco claims he's going to late-night practices and that it's normal for the female masseuse to be in the locker room with them. I'm trying to decide if my prenup can be activated. What do you think, girls, is that crazy?"

"Hell no!" said an older woman, rearing her head back adamantly. "I'm so sick of worrying about the late nights and the hang-ups."

"I just got Jennette into that private nursery school on Fifth Avenue," said a pretty woman named Tiffani, who was standing next to Angel. She put a hand to her chest and said, "I don't want to know nothing. I'm getting my girls into the best prep schools in the city, and that's that. My dad worked at a gas station, and I barely made it out of high school. My husband knows he better not mess this up for our babies."

"Honey, you have nothing to worry about. He is one of the good ones."

"I think so, too. I'm just not going to go out of my way to disprove it. I take care of the family and run the foundation while he grinds it out on the field," said Tiffani. "One of these days I'm going to open a shoe store, but for right now what we have works. I am not going to peer too closely under the hood."

"I get you. Being drama-free is nice, when you can get it. By the way, I'm looking forward to the foundation's fashion show. When are invites going out?"

"Hopefully next week. Kinley, are you going?" Tiffani asked.

"Are you joking? Of course!" the hostess exclaimed. "Do you have the models lined up?"

"Yes, Regina helped with that. She's even going to be on the runway. She wants to wear Oliver's new line. Who was I to say no?" Tiffani glanced at Angel. "Sorry, I know that's uncomfortable to bring up."

Angel, surprised at being added into the conversation, was confused for a second, then realized they were talking about Regina, Duke's ex-girlfriend. "Oh, no, it's fine. His past personal life is his business." Even as she said it, and knew she had no claim on him whatsoever, she felt a twang of jealousy.

Kinley nodded approvingly. "If we had to avoid bringing up ex-girlfriends in this crowd, we'd have some pretty quiet nights. Best if you get used to it now. Besides, if you and Duke get serious, the press isn't going to make it easy on you. They turn everything into a story line for a soap opera, creating drama where there isn't any. For sure, they will pit you and Regina against each other, as if there's some big battle brewing."

"Should I be preparing for battle?"

Everyone's head swung around at the same time. Angel's nerves were instantly on fire. There was Regina, the supermodel. The woman famously caught on camera last year calling Duke a loser and then slapping a glass of beer out of his hand, almost knocking him off a pair of crutches. Angel was terrified of the stern, willowy woman with no trace of body fat, stunning in a see-through flapperesque dress, shimmering black strands swinging around her thin, taut thighs. It was far too easy to picture Duke's hand resting there.

The women moved to her like flowers to the sun.

There was a flurry of air-kisses and squeals. Angel stood awkwardly to the side, trying her hardest to keep a confident, relaxed stance, her chin up. *I will project Zen if it kills me.*

The pack around the model broke open. Regina zeroed in on Angel. "Hello," she purred, offering a hand as if Angel should curtsy and kiss the ring.

"Nice to meet you. I'm Angel."

"Yes. And I'm Regina." The woman smirked.

Angel simply nodded, once. She couldn't read Regina's energy. She didn't want to be nice if the woman was about to throw shade.

"You are lovely in red, by the way."

"Thank you." Angel let her guard drop a little.

"Awfully nice of you to loan out your closet, Kinley," the model cooed to her friend. "I mean, the *Balmain*? You are very generous."

The blood drained from Angel's face. The ever-present hostility residing in her veins moved from a pale pink to burning red in a flash. She locked eyes with Regina, refusing to flinch. She thought Duke had sent it to her, as a gift. She turned to Kinley. "You? I didn't know . . . I assumed . . ."

Regina grabbed a glass from a passing waiter, letting her comment hang.

You are an adult. Don't throw punches.

"I sent the invitation so last minute," Kinley said smoothly, flashing a disapproving look at Regina. "I thought it only fair I send over a dress."

"I thought the invitation came from Duke." *If I could fall through a crack in the floor, I would.*

"Oh, it did. The invitation came from both of us. I told him I'd take care of the details. And here you are. It worked out perfectly, even with only a few moments' notice. You were really a good sport to work us into your schedule." Kinley fluttered her hands, elegant and gracious. "I know you're busy with school and work."

Angel felt her blue collar light up and flash neon, despite Kinley's kindness. "Thank you," she said again, low, hating that everyone knew she was only here because of Kinley's pity.

A few of the women appeared delighted at the tension Regina had created, leaning in for a catfight. But Angel really, really wanted to stay cool. *If I let her know she's getting to me, she wins. Fuck that.* She blinked slowly. *Visualize peace.*

Not everybody was comfortable letting the conflict rise. Tiffani said loudly, "I have tried to get Kinley to loan me that dress, Angel. But now I see it on, I realize I wouldn't look nearly as good as you. You've got the perfect bootie. And my mama jugs would not stay perky under those straps. Enjoy it while you got 'em."

Kinley nudged her friend, saying, "Oh, stop it! You and your mama jugs are gorgeous." Then she scanned Angel up and down. "Regina is right; you are lovely in red. I love that shade. Which reminds me . . . Tiffani, whatever happened to that red Vera Wang gown you wore to the New

Year's Eve ball a few years ago? If you're not going to wear it again, I'd love to borrow it for my trip to Croatia next week."

Kinley is a master. Angel appreciated the two women derailing Regina's comment, even if they were only trying to maintain decorum. Regina clearly did not have the same attitude. Without knowing anything about Angel, she'd come over and dropped a grenade into the conversation. *Now I know what to look out for—toothpicks bearing bombs. Why am I taking this shit? That's right—I don't have to.*

Angel smoothed a hand over her hair, adopting a hint of posh into her voice. "Croatia? I had some friends go there a few years ago and claim it was the new Hawaii," she said to Kinley. "Have you been?"

Regina answered for the hostess, her Upper East Side accent drawn out and bored-sounding. "Yes, of course we have. But are you sure you're thinking of Croatia? It's nothing like Hawaii. More like the new Monaco—but your friends wouldn't know that, would they?"

"Regina . . ." Kinley let out a loud sigh.

"Well, that's true," said Angel, purposefully planting a small smile on her lips instead of shoving the condescending C-bag against the wall. "They were with Nurses Without Borders, on a supply run from Bosnia. They were happy just to have freshwater and to not have to watch for land mines."

"That's right, I'd heard you were a nurse."

"Almost. I take my boards next week."

"Sounds . . . fascinating," said Regina, peering down at her nails, her voice trailing off.

"Yes, fascinating," tittered a young girl in the group.

Lambeojo! Angel cursed at the girl internally, flashing a dark look at the level-ten ass kisser.

"Oh, my aunt was a nurse!" one of the other women cut in, not catching Regina's subtext. "She was in a really bad neighborhood, saw a lot of nasty stuff. She said one time there was this girl who was a vagina drug mule but she was so drunk she shoved a box of McDonald's fries up there instead of the bag of hash."

"Jesus!" said Tiffani.

"What? You know you wanna hear. Girl, I bet you've seen some stuff. Any funny stories?" The woman was full and curvy, with dreads pulled into an intricate bun, and an aura of self-awareness. Angel had liked her immediately, but even more now that she'd blown past Regina's jibes.

Angel shrugged, thinking for a second. "Well, last week at the clinic, some local bouncers brought in a guy who was totally unconscious. He'd been heckling the strippers, even took a swing at a girl as she bent over him. Instead of kicking him out, the girls roofied him and drew a big dick on his face with a permanent marker."

"No!"

"And then there's this homeless guy who comes in all the time. Once, he found a diamond ring somewhere and was so excited, he stood on a chair in the middle of the waiting room and sang "Single Ladies" to the head nurse. He sounded pretty good, too, before he fell off the chair and lost his bladder."

Regina shuddered. "Ugh. I am so glad I live in Carnegie Hill."

"Oh, I don't know. People in Carnegie Hill just overdose on better drugs and shove more expensive items up their bleached bungholes." She glared at the taller woman pointedly.

"Angel," said Duke, sliding between them. "I see you met the ladies. And Regina."

The young woman wanted to sigh in relief.

Duke tipped his head in the model's direction, but his green eyes focused on Angel. He handed her a fluted glass of champagne. He gave the student nurse a half-smile, raised his own glass in salute. "Sorry it took me so long, baby."

"Baby"? How far are we taking this dating story? As she took a sip, he put a hand lightly on her bare back. She could smell tequila rolling off of him. *Good thing he's not driving.*

"So, what do you girls think of my little *chiquita*?"

Oh, no he dinna.

"Hmm. I see you're still drinking." Regina flipped her hair.

Duke's hand at the small of Angel's back clenched, but calmly he said, "Good thing you don't need to worry about it anymore."

"Thank God for that. It's going to take an Angel to put up with your ass," Regina sneered.

Angel rolled her eyes and wondered if she could get away with smashing her glass upside the bitch's head. "Luckily, I'm fine with Duke being himself. I'm not his mommy." She tilted her face up to Duke, winked at him. "Let's get some air, *baby*, it's thick in here."

Behind them, Kinley asked Regina about the fundraiser, but the model was unresponsive. Angel could feel Regina's stare drilling into her back. Duke chuckled under his breath, his hand still on her, guiding her away. *I should have unleashed on her.* These people were never going to be her friends, there was no reason to play nice.

Duke grabbed two more drinks from a passing waiter and led her through French doors to the patio, out into the comforting twinkle of candles and the Manhattan skyline.

"This is amazing," Angel breathed. In and out, calming her heart rate. She focused on the lights. She'd never seen the city like this, from such a place of privilege.

Duke stood close to her but removed his hand from her back, not wanting to freak her out. She smelled like a tart cherry pie—it was hard not to grab her and lick those luscious lips. "Thank you for what you said to Regina. That you like me when I'm being myself. Even as part of this Angel and Duke Show, that's nice to hear."

He realized as he was saying it how pitiful and insecure he sounded. *Why am I begging for compliments?* He took a gulp from his glass and stared out at the stars, so far away and untouchable. Were they real?

Angel raised an eyebrow. "When I first met you, I thought you were a regular guy. I honestly liked our conversation at the park, and watching you play with the kids, when I thought you were a construction worker or a delivery driver. Funny thing is, I think you were being the real you. Regina, though—*la puta estupida*. She's a snotty bitch, to the core."

He slugged back more of his drink and sighed, peering into the glass. Angel's words made him warm, but the mention of Regina brought him back down. *She is a bitch, but maybe not wrong about the booze.* "I know," he said. "She's always been an A-one mean girl, but she was nice enough to me, in the beginning. Until I got hurt and couldn't play. Or make money. She left when I was at my lowest." He sucked his teeth. "Sorry to drag you into this. I didn't know she'd be here tonight. Kinley should have said something."

"I think Kinley assumed we'd act like adults and stay civil. That's not my strong suit," Angel said, the gold flecks in her brown eyes twinkling. He was sorry when her brow furrowed as she continued. "Speaking of Kinley . . . She said this dress was from her. When Aaron dropped it off at my apartment, he said it was from you. I didn't appreciate Regina loudly pointing out I was wearing a borrowed dress, but I'm glad I know, so I can give it back. You should have told me."

"I didn't think about it." *I would love to have bought you that dress. Hot damn, girl.* His eyes traveled up her sleek brown legs, her curved hips, and her full breasts. *I'd love to get her into that lingerie boutique in midtown . . .*

His phone beeped with an incoming text. He ignored it, but the phone beeped again.

"Sorry," he said. He opened the message and his heart sank when he read the text:

You fired me, but your doctor doesn't know that. He called, wants more money. We need to talk. I'll be home tomorrow.

It was from his father.

Duke didn't want to think about money at this moment. He wanted life to be simple. He wanted to take the night off, enjoy the party and this fine woman beside him. But he couldn't put off the doctor; there was too much at stake.

"I hate to be rude, but I'm gonna have to call my pops back. Do you mind?"

Angel shrugged. "It's okay. I'll call Jose. I'll be back in a minute."

As she sauntered past him, he watched her hips wrapped in the red dress he wished he'd bought her—he could have watched her try it on. And slip it off.

Chapter Fourteen

Wading through the crowd of beautiful people, she spied Regina on the far side of the room, leaning against the fireplace with one foot elegantly propped on the wall behind her, a martini glass in hand. The pose was reminiscent of a famous picture of a real flapper, and Angel was sure Regina knew it.

At the door, she found the older manservant who'd taken her coat when they'd arrived. "May I please have my cell phone? You have it tucked away with a white fur stole I wore in."

"Of course, miss. Right away." The man, who probably answered to the name Jeeves, strode away.

"What do you think of our butler?" Roland towered above her.

"I didn't know there were still butlers around. I expected him to answer me in a British accent."

Roland smirked. "Steven has been with Kinley's family since he was a child, when his father was butler. Kinley talked old Steven into moving up here from Virginia when we decided to buy this monstrosity. Pissed off her parents, but they can't stay mad at their little Kinney Poo."

Kinley was walking up behind Roland. She'd heard everything. The hostess rolled her eyes at Angel and then tapped her husband on the shoulder.

"Really, Roland?"

Angel wondered if there was a way to disappear into the wall.

Roland shrugged. "Babe, you know how I feel about having Steven around."

"Uh-huh. And I know how you feel about this house, and my family . . . Maybe, just once, you could keep it to yourself. Sorry, Angel."

"It's okay—"

The butler returned. "Here you are, miss. I can put it back when you're done, if you like. Will there be anything else?"

"Alright, Steven, move along." Roland flapped a hand at him, shooing away the older man like a child. The butler didn't say a word as he returned to his post.

"You are testing me, husband," Kinley growled.

I think he's really testing poor old Steven, who I hope is using Roland's toothbrush to clean the toilet. Angel edged away and held up the phone. "I need to call home. Don't mean to be rude."

As she turned, out of the corner of her eye, she saw Roland grab Kinley's arm, glaring down at the smaller woman and jerking her roughly. Angel could hear their furious whispers, until she moved far enough away.

Asshole. He'd seemed so nice earlier, kind to his wife and mingling with the guests. The newspapers touted him as a sweetheart, one of those players everyone loved. She was disappointed to witness the truth behind the legend.

Gabriela answered the phone on the first ring. She and Jose were eating popcorn and watching *The Bachelor.*

"You have got to be kidding me, Gabriela. First of all, he better have his homework done, and second of all, what?"

Her Dominican neighbor chuckled. "Girl, go have fun. Jose is learning about women."

In the background, she heard the seven-year-old ask, "Are those spiders on her eyes? And how come she keeps crying? I thought she knew it was a game. I'd hate to play Sorry with her."

"See?" Gabriela said to Angel. "He loves it. How's it goin' with you? Who's the most famous person you've talked to? How's your hair holdin' up?"

She talked with them for a minute, telling Jose to be good and get to bed soon, then hung up. As she did, a text message flashed onto her screen.

This is Dr. Collins. Can you come in tomorrow? We need to talk.

The message disturbed her. He must have gone into her records to find her number. What could he possibly want, especially at this time of night? She considered texting him back, but decided she'd rather live with the mystery. Whatever it was, it could wait until tomorrow. She was not in the mood for his overt sexual harassment. If he thought she was around, he'd probably start sexting her.

She gave her phone to old Steven for safekeeping. Then she squared her shoulders, took a sip of her drink, and reentered the fray. Duke waved her over to where he was, at the bar. The bartender was lining up shots of tequila. Kinley was with him, but Roland had disappeared.

"Did you happen to see my husband?" she asked Angel, throwing back a shot. There were red fingerprints on her forearm.

Angel shook her head, not trusting herself to say anything.

Kinley ground her teeth. "That bastard better hide." She threw back another shot of tequila, then removed a small glass tube from between her breasts. "You want a bump?" The hostess tapped a line of coke along the top of her closed fist and sniffed.

Angel blinked. The TV star had just made a series of public service commercials about drug abuse. The money from her appearances probably paid for the powder.

"Come on, Kinley," said Duke. "You know I don't party like that no more. Besides, I get drug tested next week. You tryin' to get me in trouble?"

"I wasn't asking you." She held out the vial to Angel.

Angel hedged, not wanting to sound like a country mouse. "I can't. Once I start, I'm afraid I won't stop."

She hoped the petite woman could maintain, with that much booze and drugs kicking around inside her. *She has so little body fat, how can she not be sick?* She liked Kinley. She didn't want to see this dignified person she admired get sloppy and stupid.

Scanning the room, she scrutinized the rest of the wealthy and the famous. Were they all messed up? She pictured herself living in a fabulous house, maybe even with a maid, never worrying about scraping together a balanced meal so her kid wouldn't get scurvy or praying the check to the electric company didn't bounce. Did she want to have what they had? Be like them?

I'd like to give it a whirl, she thought. *I wouldn't let it change me.*

"Do you want another drunk?" Duke paused, then realized what he'd said. "I mean, drink?"

"I've still got this one, but thanks."

He hoped Angel was having a good time, despite Regina's presence.

He'd tried calling his father, but of course Willis didn't answer. *That'd be too easy.* Duke finally resorted to texting back, telling him to do what it took to pay the doctor and they'd work it out tomorrow. *I can't let Dr. Collins talk to reporters. Here's to hoping Pops took care of him.*

The music suddenly changed, became louder. His

mood lightened. He was ready to dance, let off some steam and watch Angel move those hips and shake that ass. Looking at her glistening skin and alert eyes, he suddenly had a strong urge to unpin her hair and run his fingers through it, let her long curls fly around free. *She finer than every woman in here.*

"Is that actually Taylor Swift up there singing?" Angel's pixie face lit up with amusement. He realized, then, that it wasn't just that she was beautiful and sexy—she also had a spark in her that burned brighter than most. She was present, ready to live. He wanted someone real, not afraid to stay real. Someone like Angel.

Kinley reached over and refilled Angel's champagne without asking, nodding her chin toward the famous singer. "That girl! Taylor's always going to be on the stage in the end. Just ask Kanye. But Roland adores her, so . . ." She shrugged.

"You have to admit, she can be catchy," Angel said. Duke's heart thumped as she twitched her shoulder to the music and grinned up at him, her lips parted and glossy. *Jesus, I'm like a middle school kid around her.*

"Well, come on then, let's get all *Risky Business* up in here." He softly tugged her to where a makeshift dance floor had formed in front of the blond pop star, who riled up the crowd with an extended version of her latest hit.

Angel slid off her high heels and held them as she

and Duke shimmied and shook. He lost himself in the pulse of the music and the energy of the people around him. He watched as Angel closed her eyes, letting her body become loose, in tune. She raised her arms, moving them gracefully, and turned to the stage, singing along. She was sexy and free. Duke wanted to close his eyes and join her.

Just then, without looking back, she pushed her backside into him, swaying her hips to the beat. He matched her rhythm, pressing against her, moving to the music together.

Then pain spiked through his ankle.

Of fucking course. He'd been moving carefully, but he'd become distracted by Angel.

He bent so his lips were on her ear and said, "Hey, I've got to sit down. My ankle doesn't feel that great." It was hard to straighten back up, not because of his balance but because of her spicy sweet smell and the slipperiness of her back.

She turned and went to take his arm, concern etched on her face.

"Stop! I don't need a nurse," he said in a low, stern voice, pushing her hand away. He scanned the crowd around him, making sure no one was paying attention.

The young woman recoiled. "Fine," she spit out.

"Don't be so sensitive," he groaned. Her face darkened further. Duke felt a surge of defensive irritation. "I meant,

I don't want these guys to see me hobbling around. I'll be fine."

He walked stiffly back to the bar and leaned against it. "Yo, another shot of tequila over here." He turned to Angel, whom he could feel standing behind him, judging him.

"You want something, Angel?"

"No, I'm good."

It was clear she was put off, which only made him more irritated. He could feel the liquor running trails through his mind; he'd been hoping she'd flow with him tonight.

She leaned against the bar, staring at him. Then she stooped to slide on her high heels, her fingers trailing across her foot and up her calf, and he forgot about his bad mood.

So damn sexy.

Kinley and a small group of women clustered around them.

"Duke, you remember Tyrone's wife, Alise?"

The wife of the current heavyweight boxing champion stepped between him and Angel, nestling up to Duke. He put a friendly arm around her, wondering if it would make Angel jealous. Hoping.

The older woman purred, "Ready for the season? Your pitching arm warmed up?"

He flexed, turning to make sure Angel could see.

"Check out these guns." His muscles bulged under his fitted white dress shirt.

A couple of the women squeezed his popped muscles, oohing and aahing, but Angel simply hoisted her glass at him. "Impressive," she said, her eyebrow arched.

"Oh, Duke, you must be so excited. It's almost time for you to start playing again, isn't it?" one of the younger women asked—the girlfriend of a rookie who was already at spring training.

He turned up the charm. "I'm a playa all the time, am I right?"

She giggled. "I guess. For an old guy."

"Ooh, ouch. Kicked me right in the nuts with that one."

"Well, a hot old guy . . . Does that make you feel better?"

"Almost as good as if you had that hot little ass pressed against me."

It was like out of a cartoon, the silence that followed. He could swear a needle screeched across a vinyl record and a circle of faces whipped from Duke to Angel and back.

He shook his head, trying to clear the tequila mist. *What? Just tryin' to be funny . . .*

Angel. He'd just shamed her. His ma would spit on him if she could.

"Bartender!" he barked.

•   •   •

Angel shook the door handle in frustration. It was locked. The bathroom in the entry hall was occupied. She almost hitched up the red dress and kicked the intricately carved door with her expensively clad foot, but she controlled herself at the last second. She also stopped herself from launching a flurry of punches at the wall or, better yet, at Duke. She wasn't going to hurt her hands or toes over a douche bag.

Angel went into the massive kitchen, an orderly bee-hive of activity by black-vested workers filling trays and washing glasses. A staff member, after removing withered mushrooms from the oven, pointed to a hallway off to the side when she asked him about a restroom. The corridor was wider than her living room and opened onto a laundry room, pantry, and what she guessed was a suite of rooms for servants. Pushing open the door to what she assumed was the bathroom, she immediately regretted it.

Regina sat on the edge of a bathtub, leaning back, her dress up around her waist, pencil-thin legs spread wide. "Mmm-mmmm." Her eyes were shut, lips puckered.

Clutching Roland Smith's short, tight curls, she was holding his head down. The married ballplayer was on his knees, his tongue lapping noisily between Regina's thighs.

"Oh, yesss. Fuck me with your tongue. Fuck me."

Before Angel could unfreeze herself, she saw Roland bob his head, up down, up down, jamming his tongue into Regina.

I'm being punished. I don't get to have sex, but I have to see it wherever I go. She started to back out. *And how come people can't lock the fucking door?*

Regina's eyes popped open and landed on her.

"Get out!" the model shrieked.

Chapter Fifteen

Angel slammed the bathroom door.

My God, I hate these people.

Duke's friend was getting it on with Duke's ex-girlfriend. In a bathroom, like teenagers at a warehouse rave. What if it had been Kinley who'd walked in? Maybe it was a good thing the hostess was coked up.

I'm out. I am out.

In the entry hall, money-bought beauty dripped down the gilded walls. Angel searched for old Steven so she could get her stuff and leave this ugliness behind.

"Sir, I'm sorry to bother you again, would you mind getting my wrap and phone? I'm leaving."

"Yes, miss. Would you like me to call you a car?"

She nodded gratefully.

"And you, sir? Am I retrieving your jacket, as well?" The butler addressed someone over her shoulder.

"Jacket? No . . . Angel, what are you doing?" Duke swayed once and then caught himself on the wall beside her. "Are you going?"

"Yes—"

A yowl broke them apart. "How dare you?" It was Regina, her black flapper dress back in place, beads swinging with her furious strides. "You little whore!"

"Excuse me?" Angel could not have been more shocked if zombies had dropped through the ceiling and started eating people.

Regina raised her hand, slicing the air before Angel realized what was happening. The model's paper-thin palm made solid contact with Angel's cheekbone, the slap ringing off the marble floors and rocking her head back.

"You mad? Your dead ass goin' down!" Angel lunged for Regina, intent on breaking her in half. Duke clumsily pushed Angel away, however, before she could make full body contact with his ex-girlfriend.

She was able to scrape her nail's down Regina's arm. She dug in savagely.

Regina screamed as if Angel had stabbed her. If only, Angel thought.

"Stop this! Stop this right now!" Kinley rushed up to them, glassy-eyed and wobbly.

Duke held Angel back while Regina cowered behind Kinley, as if she was the victim.

The hostess, slurring and confused, asked, "What's going on?"

Angel considered biting Duke's arm, to get him to let her go. "She was—"

"I just caught Angel fucking Roland in the bathroom!" Regina screamed, sobbing and holding her arm as if it was broken.

Angel stopped struggling against Duke. "What? What did you say? Are you *crazy?*"

Kinley squinted her eyes at Angel, pain blooming in waves across her face. "How could you?"

"That is not what happened! Regina—"

"Duke, take away your piece of trash!" The model's voice was shrill, hurting Angel's head more than the slap.

He grabbed her harder, physically moving her farther away from Regina, treating her as a rag doll.

A circle of partygoers crowded around the door, watching the action.

"Where's Roland?" Kinley asked, her skin mottled with distress. She focused her bloodshot eyes on Angel. "I think you better go."

"Get your fucking hands off me!" Angel tore away from Duke's grip; he was too drunk to hold her in place any longer. "You people are goddamn nuts. Fucking certifiable." Angel grabbed her fur and phone from old Steven, who was standing off to the side, proper and impassive, though she saw pity flash through his eyes. She rushed into the open elevator, mortified. No one followed, not even

Duke. He simply stood there, dumbfounded, as the doors slid shut.

Chest heaving, she stared into the mirrored walls, at the red handprint on her face and Duke's angry fingerprints on her upper arms. *Kinley and I will have matching bruises tomorrow*, she thought, as the elevator plummeted to the ground. Her mind couldn't find a place to rest. *This is a nightmare. It has to be.* She had done nothing wrong. Nothing. Except agree to put herself out there for someone else. Never again. *It's me and Jose from now on. That's it.*

Out on the street, her skin pebbled with cold. She didn't feel it. Her blood ran hot. Stalking away from the building, passing under a row of richly colored awnings, she realized she had no way to pay for the town car that old Steven had called for her, especially not for a ride from Central Park to Mount Eden in the Bronx. She didn't have enough for an Uber to go that distance.

She ran a hand over her hip, the four-thousand-dollar dress slick under her palm. On Park Avenue, she blended in. The women passing her were decked out in sexy, hip haute couture and bling. The men were in black suits, and liveried doormen were on every block. Jazzy blues floated free from high-end restaurants, and the blooming lavender and rosemary bushes in the sidewalk planter boxes competed with car exhaust. She hated all of it. She blinked, hoping to be magically transported to her own neighborhood, where it smelled like urine, oil, and home-cooked foods, and the hanging laundry overhead snapped in the wind. And the people were real.

Angel drew the fur over her cleavage, keeping an eye out for a bus stop. *I bet I'll be the best-dressed woman using public transportation tonight.* She debated taking off her shoes—her feet were killing her—but gagged at the thought of her bare flesh on the disease-ridden pavement. Park Avenue might look clean, but it was just as dirty as the Bronx.

She almost jumped out of her skin when someone tapped her on the shoulder.

It was Duke.

"Don't sneak up on me like that!"

"I wasn't—"

"Get away from me!"

He seized her forearm, swinging her around. His face was intense as he towered over her. "Come on—"

She went white-hot with rage.

"Let me go!" She tried ripping her arm free, but his grip was too strong. An enraged sob burst free. "You're hurting me!"

And then she jammed her thousand-dollar spike heel into the top of his uninjured foot, where the shoe met the sock.

"Ow!" He let go. "Damn it, that hurt! I am just trying to talk to you."

"That's the second time you've put hands on me tonight." Tears were fluttering on her lashes. "You guys. You're all alike. Talking with your fists."

"I wasn't trying to hurt you, just—"

"Really? What's this." She thrust her arm between them, revealing the red marks marring the skin on her upper and lower arm from where he'd grabbed her earlier. "Stay away from me."

"I didn't mean—I promise, I won't—"

"What? You won't do it again? Yeah, that's what Jose's father would say, too. It's what my father would tell my mother."

His face twisted with horror. "No. That's not me." He backed away from her. Abruptly, he folded his body down onto the yellow curb. "This whole night is fucked," he mumbled, his head hanging. "I can't believe you'd do me like that," he muttered.

"You son of a bitch." Angel swung on her heel and marched down the pavement.

"Hey! Hey! Stop," he yelled after her, slightly slurry. "I thought you were different!"

She did not look back.

He watched her go. *What am I doing wrong here? How come I can't get my shit together?*

"Cigarette, bro?"

It was Roland. The tall ballplayer kept back a few steps, shamefaced.

"What in the fuck? That was my girl, man. So not right." Duke lumbered partway to his feet, then let his body drop back to the curb, too exhausted and sore to go after a beast like Roland. *Not tonight.*

His friend squinted at him. "Your girl? You serious? Anyway, I wasn't bangin' that nurse."

"What?" Duke took a second to process the response. "Then why'd Regina say that?"

Roland shrugged, taking a long draw on his cigarette. The cherry burned bright orange, lighting up his thousand-yard stare.

Duke slitted his eyes at him. "But you did get it on with somebody. You was cheating at Kinley when she twenty feet away? I hope she dumps your ass."

The big man sank down next to him on the curb, his long legs splayed into the street. "Dude. I know. The woman's gonna stick a knife in my throat when she sees me. I'm gettin' a hotel until she cools down."

"If she cools down. You fucking deserve to get shut out."

"Oh, and you're Mister Hun' Percent?"

They sat quietly, two professional athletes beaten down by their own bad habits.

"You goin' after her? The nurse?"

"She doesn't want me to. I tried." *Like an asshole.*

"Prob' for the best. Women are nothing but trouble."

Duke felt his mood shift from depressed to defensive. "Not her. I had to beg Angel to come here. I don't get what

Regina is playin' at. I should never have believed her. Angel isn't like that." He slapped a hand to his head. "She isn't." Duke leapt up. "What am I doin'? I can't let her walk around alone."

"Duke, I gotta say something—"

"Later." The pitcher speed-walked down the sidewalk.

Roland, from the curb, said, "Big waste of time, dude!"

This from the guy humpin' outside meat, Duke thought. He unbuttoned his jacket and elongated his stride, his suit pants uncomfortably tight on his upper leg muscles. Angel shouldn't have had to deal with Regina. *What is her fucking problem?*

A black limo drew up next to him. The driver leaned toward the open passenger window. "Sir? Steven said you'd be needing a car?"

"Perfect timing. We have to find a girl."

"How much, honey?"

The old man covered in grime was crouched at one end of the bus stop, but he scooted his skinny haunches an inch closer.

Angel stood up. "*Pendejo!*" She wrapped the fur stole around her tighter. "What makes you think I'm a hooker, dirtbag?"

"Tsk, tsk, don't be mean. That's a nice dress." He reached out a hand, as if to run his dirt-packed nails over the material. The air he stirred smelled of sour milk.

"Touch me and suffer the consequences," she snarled.

There were other people passing by; she wasn't worried about being molested. Her biggest concern was that she'd take out her night on this sad sack and someone would end up in the hospital.

He withdrew his shaky hand and folded his arms over his chest, defiant. "That's a *Balmain*, right? You don't deserve to be wearing that dress."

She cut her eyes at him in surprise. *How many homeless guys know fashion?* Looking closer, she realized that his tattered clothing was the remnants of a tuxedo, though he had a shredded wool blanket over his shoulders and plastic sandals on his gnarled feet. Before she could say any more, someone shouted her name from the street.

Duke was standing up through the moonroof of a limo, which was blocking traffic.

"Angel! I'm sorry! Let me give you a ride home!" Several cars behind the limo laid on their horns, a noisy backdrop to his pleas.

"Hell no!" She sat back down on the bench next to the homeless fashionista. "Go away."

"Come on! I'll be good, I promise!"

"No!"

"Lady, wouldja get in the car already?" a cabby with a heavy New Jersey accent yelled at her, supported by a dozen more honks.

The tuxedo guy next to her shook his white, dreaded hair. "Don't do it. You can't trust anybody these days."

Duke begged. "I know Regina lied, okay? I'm sorry!"

She sprang to her feet, barely sticking a landing with the high heels. "Oh, so now you believe me?"

"I'll explain if you get in the car." Duke's voice was calm, but his face was tense.

The old man bounced up and down on the bus stop bench, then loudly passed gas. "That's what she thinks of your offer!"

Angel rolled her eyes. Why did every man think they had a say in what she did? The smell of rotten eggs attacked her nostrils.

She marched to the car, opened the back door, and sat on the edge of the seat, glowering at him. "Take me right home. No screwing around."

Duke held up his palms in surrender. "Whatever you want, I promise." He lowered his hands, gave the driver instructions to her apartment, and turned to her. Quietly, he said, "Roland told me it wasn't you."

She gazed out the window, trying to avoid his eye contact in the reflection. "I can't believe you'd think I'd do that in the first place. Do I seem like the kind of person who sneaks off to have sex with a stranger? A married stranger?"

"No! I didn't really believe it at the time. I was . . . confused. I have no idea what games Regina is playing, but I'm sorry you were caught in the middle."

"Didn't Roland tell you?" She faced him.

"Tell me what?"

"It was Regina. He was, uh, with Regina in the bathroom."

Duke leaned his head against the seat back and took a deep breath, holding it.

"I'm sorry, Duke."

He blew out the air in a whoosh. "Poor Kinley. It's not like I have feelings for Regina—but my best friend? Why's he gotta go there?"

"Douche bag move," Angel agreed. New York's sweetheart was anything but.

Duke shut his eyes. "My whole life, my family and friends have had these high expectations for me, but not one of them seems to care about meeting the bar for being a decent human being." His words came slowly. "As a kid, I thought the better I played, people would like me more. I loved baseball when I was in school, sliding through dirt, practicing with my team before we went out for pizza. But even then, people were nice to me because I was good, not because I'm me. It's taken a while to see it's my fame they like. Even my pops."

"Not one real friend? Do you think that's true?"

"I thought Roland had my back, but he's out for himself, always. There was Mark . . ."

He grabbed a bottle of water from the bucket at his feet and drank it down in a few large gulps.

"You don't have to talk about him if you don't want to."

"It's just hard. Mark was a good guy. He had a wife and two little girls and they were the center of his world. I'd go over for Sunday night barbecues and it was like a normal night for normal guys. He was one of the best catchers the Bronx Bolts ever had, but he didn't spend a lot of time talking about it or trying to prove himself. I craved what he had. He was so comfortable with who he was, and he had a loving family who adored him."

"Mark sounds like he was a stand-up friend. My friend Gabriela is like that for me, but we're both too busy to talk much. She gets to see Jose more than I do, but thank God he has her." She tucked a strand of hair behind her ear. "I have to admit, I've never felt like you—that I've disappointed someone—but, then again, I've never had anyone to disappoint. Except Jose. It's just been me and Jose for a long time now. Which is fine. I don't have time to try and please people. I got to keep myself on point or Jose suffers."

"You're a good mom."

"I don't know about that, but I try to be a good person. I'd never do what Roland did to you, or his wife. And I don't know what's up with your father, but you should find yourself some better friends."

The limo turned onto Jerome Avenue, a few blocks from her house.

"You're right, I definitely need a higher class of people in my life. What are you doing right now?"

She laughed. "It's late! I've got to get Jose up and out the door for school in the morning. And Gabriela is not going to want to hang out on my couch for much longer."

"Come on, it's only ten thirty. I bet if you asked Gabriela, she'd be fine. Why don't you call her."

Gabriela would ask if I had a condom and give me tips on different positions. She'd have no problem with Angel staying out late. But should she?

"Um, don't take this the wrong way, but why should I trust you?"

His face paled, not out of anger but out of mortification. Taking her arm gently, he ran a thumb over one of the fading red streaks that his grip had left earlier. There probably wouldn't be much bruising, but there would be bruising on the inside, for them both.

"If you mean physically, you have every right to ask me that, but I swear to God I've never hurt a woman. I was drunk. I shouldn't have grabbed you. I was just trying to hold you back, but I should not have done that. It won't happen again."

"And what about emotionally? We come from different places. Do you think we can really be friends? Honestly, why would you want to be friends with me, anyway? I'm just a bartending nurse, remember?" I mean, really, how is it that a sad Bronx Bolt pitcher is asking me if I'll be his friend? Can this night get any weirder? It definitely can get better.

He wrapped his fingers lightly around hers. "You are the best person I know. Let's just hang out, no pressure, I'll have the driver take you back when you're ready."

"Take me back from where?"

"Let's go to my house. I will be the perfect gentleman. And I make a mean homemade pizza."

She caught her breath. Is that what she wanted? For him to be a gentleman? Maybe not.

Within a few minutes, the limo drove up to a large, modern house. Angel leaned forward to get a better view and was impressed with the sleek wood-and-glass front, a Scandinavian appeal.

Angel's id was producing second thoughts. *I should have the car take me home right now. We've both had too much to drink.* But her ego liked having a man at her side. This hot, hot man. Even if it was just for the night. *Use him, like he's been using you with the press,* she reminded herself. *He's leaving, so this is a no-strings-attached deal. Perfect. No one gets hurt.*

Duke interrupted her thoughts. "Oh, thank God. My pop's car is gone. He'd pour you a snifter of my best brandy and tell you how important he is while massaging your shoulders. Ignoring me the whole time, of course, since we're not talking to each other."

Duke helped her out. Walking to the double front doors, she said, "Your dad is *that* guy, huh?"

"He's . . . interesting. And we are not getting along right now. I may or may not have fired him today." He caught her glance and shrugged. "Long story. It'll be fine."

They went inside. Duke's home was classy and comfortable, not fussy. Clean-lined without being sterile. "This is beautiful, Duke."

"Thanks. My ma picked it out, actually, long before we had any money." He walked her through the entry room, a study, and a large living area. "When I was little, she and I would spend Sundays driving around nice neighborhoods, pointing out the places we'd buy when we made it big. We both liked this one." He stopped to light a candle on a side table. He kept talking, but his tone turned a shade darker. "A few years ago, I bought it and had it renovated. I tore the motherfucker right down to the beams. Made something new and different. Then I moved in."

He leaned against a wall, crossed his arms. Angel cocked her head to the side, studying him. She could understand the need to tear something down and start over. But maybe not to that extreme.

"She'd always tell me I was going to grow up to be a big deal, that I'd play ball for the Bronx Bolts. That was her dream for me. Until she was gone."

"And here you are. What happened to her? Did she pass away?"

"No. She got tired of cleaning up after my pop's gambling and cheating. When I started to get in trouble in middle school, she told me I was throwing away my gifts, that I was ugly inside . . . that I was a loser, just like Pops. Then she left."

Angel was quiet for a minute. She was glad Jose had never known his father and so could not be hurt by him. She could easily picture Duke as a child. To be abandoned by his mother? After all she'd heard tonight, her heart ached for him.

"Do you talk to her now?"

"No. She left. I'm not letting her back in, even if she wants it."

"She was wrong, Duke. You're beautiful, inside and out." She blushed but kept going. "You've made something of yourself. I mean, you're pitching for the Bronx Bolts!"

"But what happens if I can't pitch? What then? Back to being a loser."

"You said that before. Do you really think that?"

He blushed and stood up straight. "Nah. I'm just worried about getting back in shape in time." He strode over to a staircase, his limp barely noticeable. "Hey, I'm gonna run upstairs for a minute. There's a pool out back, if you want to wander around. Or, if you want anything, the kitchen's that way." He pointed. "I have a good bottle of red open on the counter, and there are wineglasses in one of the cupboards."

She watched as Duke easily mounted the stairs two at a time, despite the large amount of tequila he'd drunk earlier, and favoring one leg. His shape was certainly fine. The gray suit pants he wore were stretched taut over his flexing muscles. *The gluteus maximus muscles. I will ace that part of my anatomy test.*

In the spacious steel-and-wood kitchen, she checked her messages, sending off a quick update to Gabriela, purposefully ignoring the message from the doctor. *I'll deal with him tomorrow.*

Angel found the wine and, after some searching, spotted the wineglasses on a high shelf. She took off her fur wrap and high heels and dropped them by the table, then found a step stool to reach the glasses. She'd just mounted the top step when she heard Duke enter the kitchen.

"Be careful! That stool is not the greatest," Duke said, coming up behind her.

Angel planted her feet. "Okay, thanks." She held a glass aloft. "I hope these are the—" As she turned her torso to face him, the stool shifted. She lost her balance, tottering.

Duke leapt toward her. She toppled forward, having just enough time to utter a short scream before landing on his broad chest. His hands grasped her waist, holding her in place, her face less than an inch from his.

"Thank—"

His lips gently feathered down onto hers, pressing lightly. Seeking permission.

Bonitooo, she thought, her mind melting.

And then she dropped the wineglass.

"Oh, no! I'm so sorry!"

Bemused, he said, "No worries. But you don't have any shoes on. Here," he said, and slid an arm under her knees, another behind her back, picked her up, and carried her to the long cedar-slab kitchen table, setting her down gently on the tabletop. Her arms were round his neck, loosely, but her grip broke when he stepped away.

"Let me clean this up before you step on glass." He poured her a glass of wine and then swept.

She drank the wine too quickly, needing to place something against her lips. She watched him methodically clean up her mess, enjoying the domesticity. "You're so good at that. You'll make someone a great husband."

He raised an eyebrow. "Nice. Reverse discrimination."

She laughed. "True."

"Actually, I like to take care of my house. My last girlfriend used to say I cleaned better than her maid."

Angel winced. "Regina?"

Duke blanched. "Yeah. I shouldn't have brought her up."

"It's okay. Why did you guys break up, anyway?"

"We were never going to last, but after the shooting at the bar, I had a hard time coping. But you probably know that. The press covered every minute of it. But Regina hated that I wasn't working, and she hated having to take care of me. So she didn't. She says it was because I was drinking too much, and maybe that was partly it, but it was mostly because she could not stand when I wasn't catering to her."

Another woman who left him because he'd made a mistake or something went wrong, like his mom. This guy has some legit baggage.

He continued, sweeping the glass into a dustpan. "I'd lost a good friend and I was in a lot of pain, physically and emotionally. I wasn't able to play. I was even a suspect in Mark's shooting. I let myself go to a real dark place. I've struggled to get back on track, but I want to make it. I want to get back to my normal life, be someone again."

"Mark was your catcher, right? I remember the story

vaguely, but, I'm sorry, I haven't had a chance to read the papers much since being in school."

He carried the wine bottle back to her, where she sat on the table. "You're empty."

She didn't want any more wine, but she was happy to have him closer. The red dress had slid up her legs, leaving her thighs exposed. He noticed. She didn't cover herself.

He rubbed the bottle along the inside of her knee. The glass was cool and smooth against her skin. She shivered.

Duke moved the bottle away, plucked the glass from her hand, and placed both on the island. Before she could move, he was back, his palm replacing the smooth glass on her thigh. "Are you still mad at me?"

"Maybe a little," she said, her hand over his. *Just friends, with benefits, right?* She moved his hand higher.

"Do you think I could make it up to you?" His fingertips brushed against her flesh.

"You can try . . ."

His lips mashed down on hers, which instantly opened for him. Her tongue leapt forward, her body arching into him. His hands were in her hair, pulling her to him, kissing her hard. Angel matched him, striving to be even closer. He tore his lips away and she groaned, and then groaned again when he thumbed down the satin material crisscrossing her breasts. He took first one nipple in his mouth, and then the other, flicking her with his tongue.

She forgot who she was and how they came to be here, her mind focused down to only sensation and movement.

She slid off his shirt, his chest rock hard under her palms, her lips. In return, he gently brushed a finger back and forth across her panties. Back and forth—it was unbearable. She almost screamed. Then, with one swift move, he tugged off her underwear and pushed himself against her, the material of his slacks rough against her. She was delirious, unable to form coherent thought. It had been so long. She clawed at the closures of his pants while he unzipped her dress.

"Are you sure?" he asked, his green eyes piercing hers.

"Yes, yes!" she said, and he slid the dress up over her head. She was naked before him, lying on his table. "Yes," she moaned, and he was inside her.

Chapter Sixteen

Angel woke up to an odd sound. Silence.

Why is it so quiet? No traffic, no train, no sirens. She opened her eyes. The room was pitch-black. *Where am I?*

"Mmm-hm," came a muffled sleep-hum from next to her. She froze. Duke. It was Duke. Sound asleep in a large, comfortable bed, in a tangle of soft sheets and a goose down quilt. Naked. With her. *Dios mío.* The things he had done to her. The things she had done to him . . .

A pounding headache made thinking difficult.

The bedside clock said 3:15. Jose would be up in a couple of hours and she did not want him to know she'd had a "sleepover" with his hero. She would not build up his hopes like that.

Sliding stealthily from under warm blankets, she felt around for her bra and panties. *I cannot see a damn thing.* She patted around the nightstand next to her, where she did find her phone. After a minute of nudging around the carpet with her toes and coming up short, she decided to leave her underwear behind. A sacrifice to the sex gods.

A picture of herself and Duke from last night floated through the throb in her head. She remembered where she'd left her underwear. On the kitchen table. *As you do.*

She ran her hand over the wall until she found the door to what she hoped was the master bathroom, stepped carefully into the dark void, shut the door, and turned on the light. *Bright light!* Her brain screamed, sending a jolt of pain to the back of her eyes to let her know it wasn't pleased.

In a wall of mirrors, she saw a young woman with crazy hair, one false eyelash missing and the other dangling. And a tight body. She was surprised. She hadn't seen herself naked in a full mirror for quite some time. She ran her hand over her flat stomach, cupped her breasts. *You bangin'*, she thought, and laughed softly, *and possibly still drunk.*

She flushed and dropped her hands. Duke had spent quality time with her breasts last night, if she was to trust the river of half-images pouring through her mind.

Angel realized her only clothes were a pair of Spanx. And the dress and high heels—but she wasn't about to put those back on. She'd leave them with Duke. She had no desire to see Kinley. Checking out the mess in the mirror, she didn't really want to see Duke, either.

She spotted Duke's gym bag on a rack of metal shelves, which also held at least fifty pairs of kicks . . . Adidas, New

Balance, even some skater shoes. There were a number of Nikes, including a pair of high-tops with "The Duke" stitched in black and white thread on a shiny gold background, using the pointy Bronx Bolts team font.

Only two pairs of dress shoes, which made her smile. Digging through his gym bag, she found a stack of sweatshirts and gym shorts. She chose shorts with a drawstring and a plain black hoodie she hoped he wouldn't miss. She could have fit another person in the sweatshirt with her, but at least the volumes of material hid that she wasn't wearing a bra. There was also a pair of rubber shower sandals in the bag, the only footwear that looked to cost less than two hundred dollars. *Well, it's these or barefoot.*

She cracked open the door leading into the hall, peering to the left and right to make sure no one was around. *I've done this an awful lot in the past few days.* The hallway was empty. Phone and sandals in hand, she crept down the stairs, using the light on her cell phone as a flashlight. She found herself in the modern kitchen, facing the oversize cedar-plank table. She flushed again. Memories rushed in, slightly blurry yet immediately arousing. She paused and glanced up the stairs. *I could go back up there. I bet I could talk him into at least one more round.* Her warm loins screamed out in agreement.

No. I can't. She had to get home before Jose woke up. Last night, she'd justified every choice she made—from accepting his apology, to getting in his car, to writhing against him—all because she'd wanted to get laid. Granted, it was by the Duke, who claimed to want to be her friend . . . but still.

Time to get back on track.

There, on the back of a dining chair, was the red dress. The white stole and the expensive high heels were on the floor, thankfully both in good shape, next to her crumpled pair of Spanx. She stuffed the underwear in her pocket.

Time to run away.

She found a small pad of paper and pencil on the counter and tore off a page. Biting down on the eraser, Angel realized she had no idea what to say. She had no idea what to think. What had just happened? What should she do next?

Finally, she asked Duke to return Kinley's clothes, signing off with a weak, undeclarative, *Thanks for the party. I know you'll have a great season. XO.*

She quietly slipped outside and called a cab, arranging to be picked up down the block, at the corner. No way did she want anyone to see her leaving Duke's house in the middle of the night, but especially not wearing oversize athletic clothes and carrying a fur stole. She was dressed like, well, like she'd had sex all night. Taxis felt safer than Uber, since there were no computer apps tracking her.

She could survive a walk of shame to the corner, as

long as it was quick and in the dark and there were no paparazzi. And as long as she got home before Jose woke up.

She stepped out from under the portico, let her eyes adjust to the night. A heavy February mist clung to her skin, like stepping into a steam room. A steam room that was only forty degrees. She shivered and walked four or five steps, sliding around in the large, rubbery sandals. Sighing in frustration, she kicked the sandals off and tossed them back in the direction of the door. She jogged down Duke's long drive, barefoot after all.

Even Cinderella had one shoe. And a bra.

Diagnoses, Doses, Delusions, Doctors, Do not resuscitate . . .

Angel's studying led back to the Ds, time after time.

Drunk. Duke.

The school's library was chilly, raising goose bumps on her arms, even though she was wearing a thick cardigan. *I hate early spring. Wet and filled with hope—a hope that too often gets rained out.*

Her phone ringer was off. She wanted to stay happy and content a while longer. She'd made it home in time for a quick nap, and then she'd gotten Jose quietly off to school. She'd left a note for Gabriela, who was still asleep on her couch. Angel was glad she didn't wake up. She wasn't ready to share the night with anyone else, not just yet.

Angel finished reading and highlighting her notes

from anatomy. *Do I go over these again? So much to do.* She sighed and removed a slim binder from her backpack. She was not ready to dive back into the reality of her research paper, but the final draft was due.

A white paper cup was placed on the table in front of her, steam rising into the bookish air.

"Hi," said a strong, melodious voice.

She nearly got whiplash, jerking her head up. "Duke!" she said, earnest joy spreading across her face before she could control it.

"Gabriela told me I'd find you here."

"I—I don't—"

"I know. I had a great time, too."

She giggled. Like a child. For the first time in years. *Oh, please bend down and kiss me.* Instead, he pushed the coffee toward her and took a seat.

"I wanted to apologize again about last night. They were awful to you. I was awful to you."

"I remember a few times last night that were pretty okay," she said, turning fire-engine red.

He laughed. "I remember a few times you . . . Never mind. Anyway, I was hoping you didn't leave because you sobered up and realized you hated me." He was so earnest, like a nervous little boy. "But I'm not leaving until you give back the clothes you stole from me—just before sneaking away without saying good-bye." He folded his arms, one eyebrow arched over his sparkling eyes.

"Uh, yeah, about that." She squirmed in her chair, ashamed, but was thrilled he had sought her out. "I'm sorry. I'll get the shorts and shirt to you tomorrow. I had to get home to Jose."

He smiled, relief etched into his face. "I'm glad it wasn't because you thought you made a mistake." He picked up his coffee and sipped. "I'm not here to badger you. You have to study. Maybe I can help."

Her words tumbled out in haste, before he changed his mind. Or she changed hers. "Jeez, that would be great." She thought he could probably see her heart beating through her shirt. He smelled delicious. *Like sex and candy,* she sang to herself.

"Eh, books aren't really my thing, just so you know. But I'm here, use me." He waggled his eyebrows. Angel pictured a number of different ways she'd like to use him, none of which would help her pass her finals. *Well, maybe anatomy.* She grinned back.

"How about quizzing me on these terms?"

He read the first line. "Je-sus. *Vasovagal syncope.* That sounds nasty."

She tried not to laugh while swallowing a mouthful of hot coffee. "It means you've fainted."

"Is this Latin?"

"Some of the terms are. But maybe if you just read the first line of description to me, see if I know the name . . ."

"Okay, I can do that."

"Thank you."

"But I have to say one thing first. Remember that day you heard Roland and me talking about the ugly finder?"

She cocked her head to the side, sifting through her limited memories with this beautiful man. "Us who? Ugly what?"

"That first day at the Peacock, when you brought Roland and Aaron and me water while we were talking about my charity game, when a hitter put a foul right in the dugout. That kinda foul is called an ugly finder—"

"Yeah, okay. I remember. You were making fun of the guy who got hit."

"No, Roland was making fun . . . Anyway, I've been thinking. You're my ugly finder."

"I—Huh?"

The Duke laughed. "You found my ugly and you knocked it right out of me."

For the next twenty minutes, the pitcher from the Bronx Bolts sat with her in the musty library and peppered her with question after question. He kept his hat low, slouched in a chair with his ankle propped on a chair. He was wearing the gold high-tops with his name stitched on them, but with his back to the room he was anonymous in a sea of students.

Angel knew who he was. The famous guy who'd given her four orgasms the night before.

"I know you have other things to do. You don't have

to spend your day with me, not like this. I'm sure you're bored out of your mind."

"Come on, I know your test is in a few days." He put down a stack of flash cards. "I can't stay forever, but I want to help. Though I have to go as soon as my idiot father calls back." He rubbed his foot against her calf under the table, sending a thrill up her leg. "You are totally kicking ass! You're a pro when it comes to memorization. I'm impressed. I couldn't remember any of this stuff."

"That is so not true. You must have to memorize plays and calls and everybody from the other teams and how they bat . . . I think you're selling yourself short."

"Eh, that's easy stuff. Believe me, you are a superstar. I'm proud to know someone as smart and hardworking as you. You make me want to go to college."

"What would you study?"

He put his finger along his chin and squinted into the distance, the classic thinking-man pose. "I never liked school. I only stayed for the sports. I was drafted right out of high school, so college never even entered my mind. I'm not good at much else other than playing ball."

"I seriously doubt that is true. What's something you like to do, other than baseball?"

"Basketball?"

"Ha, you're hilarious."

"I guess I like coaching kids. It's been in the back of my mind that when I retire I'll probably coach a Little League team or somethin'."

"I could see you coaching. Jose and his team loved you. I don't know if you have to go back to school for that."

"I think I'd like to take a few basic teaching courses, so I would understand more of how their little brains work. Maybe I'd even take a finance class, figure out how to manage a business. My dad has really fucked things up for me."

"Hi, Angel."

It was Theresa, her arms loaded with books. "Do you mind if I sit here?" Then she saw Duke's face under the bill of his hat and her pink lips became an O. She picked up the books she had set down. "I'm sorry, I didn't realize . . ."

"No, no, stay. He's helping me study."

"Aren't you the—"

"Shh."

"Oh, right, of course." Theresa was flustered for a second. She leaned forward and stage-whispered, "I didn't recognize you the other day, but everyone knew who you were by the time you left! I had no idea you and Angel were dating!" Then she took out a notebook and pen and said normally, "What are you guys working on?"

Angel and Duke exchanged shy smiles. He was adorable when his green eyes crinkled. *Are we dating now? For real? Is that what I want?*

She said to Theresa, "I was about to make Duke quiz me on drug interactions, but you probably need to go over that, too. Duke, would you mind reading over my essay, instead? Look for obvious typos, or tell me if a sentence doesn't make sense?"

She handed him the binder with her report. He flipped it open and read for a second. "I'm not sure I'm going to be very helpful. This is intense."

"I know, it's academic, but maybe you'll spot a missing period or something."

"I'll give it a shot."

Angel and Theresa took turns asking each other questions while Duke read. Angel had to stop herself from gazing at him, because watching him read aloud under his breath, intent on the text in front of him, drove her mad. She wanted to close those moving lips with a long kiss. And then open them with her tongue.

After a few minutes, he stopped and said, "Is this for real?"

"What do you mean?"

"Are there really so many black kids dying from asthma? How come they don't have medicine that works?"

"I know, it's crazy. You'd think they'd have alternative pharmaceuticals by now," Theresa said.

"Pharma companies focus their research on improving Viagra and hair-growth medication. More people need to look into why it's happening, anyway. I mean, most of the boys on Jose's baseball team have some level of asthma kick in when they're outside playing, so I'm sure it's the air around here. But Jose's lungs get irritated sometimes just by playing in his room. The damn land-lord couldn't care less about taking care of the mold in the walls or sealing the windows so dust from the train doesn't get in."

Duke pounded a fist into his hand. "I'll talk to the motherfucker."

"Unfortunately, he's somewhere in the Florida Keys."

He exhaled a deep breath and took a sip of coffee. "How do you get scientists to start spending more time researching this?"

"You'd have to find funding."

"Huh. This is really bugging me."

"It should! You saw Jose, how bad he was two days ago. We treat asthmatic kids at the clinic all the time, sometimes really bad episodes. Some white kids, but mostly Puerto Rican and black."

He frowned deeply and went back to his reading.

Theresa whispered to Angel, "Speaking of the clinic . . . have you talked to Dr. Collins today?"

"No, not since the day before . . ." They both looked at Duke and back at each other and grinned.

"The doctor has dyed his hair black."

"Oh my God, the silver fox is trying to go back in time."

Theresa giggled. "It's the fakest thing I've ever seen. And there's a black ring around the collar of his lab coat."

"I am so glad we're almost done with that moron."

"He was bugging me about you last night, though, asking if I'd heard from you. What's that all about?"

"Oh God. I don't know. He texted and asked me to come in today. I'm putting it off as long as I can."

Angel and Theresa got out their laptops and divided a list of terms for which they needed more information. *How in the hell did people research before Google? Unless you had a good librarian, it must have taken months to find what you needed.* She was trying to figure out the difference between electrocardiography and electrocorticography when a notification bubble floated across the middle of her screen, and then another. Collecting facts might have taken forever back in the day, but at least students weren't distracted by random bullshit like Instagram pings.

Gabriela had sent her a text, and Latisha had sent a message to her Facebook inbox. *I do not have time for those gossip hounds right now.* She ignored the notifications and moved on to electromyography. But then Gabriela sent an email.

The subject line said, "Look at this asap." Gabriela's message didn't say much except "Brace yourself," and included a link to a YouTube video.

Next to her, Theresa let out a tiny gasp, almost a hiccup. Angel swiveled her head. Her neck creaked. Theresa's computer screen was on BuzzFeed. The banner dominating the page read, "The Duke hit a screaming home run with his ex-girlfriend, and we've got the sex tape to prove it. Click here."

She turned back to her own computer, to Gabriela's email. Angel hovered the mouse over the link she'd sent. Theresa, with big eyes, shook her head. Duke continued scratching notes in the margin of the essay, unaware of their nonverbal communication.

Angel couldn't help herself; she clicked.

She hit Play.

"Oh, you like that, baby?" Regina moaned, head thrown back.

On the screen, Duke couldn't answer. His mouth was full of flesh. Regina straddled him, writhing up and down. They were having sex on what looked to be a tall ottoman in front of a bank of windows.

Angel hit Pause. Regina stopped, halfway up the man pole Angel had enjoyed the night before. Regina's vagina was again making an appearance, for the second day in a row. *WTF.*

"What's that?" Duke asked from across the table, a half-smile twisting his lips. "You girls watchin' porn?"

"You. And Regina."

"No."

Theresa jumped up, swept her books and computer into her bag, her pink face pinker than usual. "I gotta go. Thanks for studying with me." Without another word, she rushed into the book stacks.

Angel did not make eye contact with Duke, only shoved her computer at him. His eyes widened.

"No way," he whispered, a low sound of horror. "I cannot believe this is happening." He shut the computer and slid it back toward her. "Angel . . ."

Angel blazed at him. "What, Duke? What do you want me to say?"

"That was last year."

"I'm not sure that matters." Her stomach ached, a thousand razors slicing into her intestines.

He shoved back from the table. "It does matter! I haven't been with her for months, and I wouldn't touch that bitch now for anything!" He crossed his arms and groaned at the ceiling. "Another scandal. This puts me sideways with the team. I'm fucked."

Refusing to feel sorry for him, she tipped her head to the computer. "Yes, you are. You were." When he glared at her, she glared back. "I do not need this in my life! You begged me to pretend to be your girlfriend, and I did it, because you were good to Jose. For my efforts, I was treated like a dog by your friends." She ran a hand through her hair, angrily, and barely restrained her yelling. "Damn it, now I look stupid and Jose's going to see me in the headlines, this time with you two and a sex tape! You did this! You clean it up. I want no part of it."

He leaned forward. "You think I want this to be happening?"

"I don't care. It's your mess. I have to think about Jose, which means passing my exams. Don't you get that?" she said, coldly. "My entire future is wrapped up in the next week. If I screw up, I might as well stick Jose and his empty inhaler in a coffin!"

Angel laid her head in her arms on the table, unable to suppress the huge emotions whirling through her.

"You're right," she heard him say. "Yeah. I don't know what I was thinkin', treading here."

Into the table, she said, "That ugly is still in you, isn't it?"

After a moment, she lifted her head. He was gone.

Alone at the library table, she had no idea how long she'd been sitting there. Hatred and fury raged through her, weighed down with sorrow and guilt.

How could I have been so stupid? I couldn't learn my lesson from dealing with the rich assholes at the Peacock? She picked up a sheet of paper covered in blue-inked lecture notes, stared at it blindly. *I have got to find a way to get him out of my head.*

The horror on his face when he saw the video was stuck in her head. She felt less sorry for him when she recalled the actual video. Or his parting words. Sounded like he was realizing he was better than her.

Oh. It struck her then—she'd done the exact same thing he'd talked about last night. The people closest to Duke pushed him away whenever something went wrong. He was not worth a second chance when he made a mistake, or so he believed, anyway. She'd just reinforced that insecurity.

After a short time fruitlessly trying to memorize terms,

she picked up her phone from where she'd left it on the table, upside down, ignoring everyone. Gabriela had texted again, but not Duke. *Of course not. I just told him to leave me the hell alone.*

He'd claimed the sex tape was made last year. When he was with Regina. If that was true, he wasn't cheating on anybody. He wasn't hurting the woman. Obviously, it had been quite the opposite. Angel swallowed down bile. She wasn't sure how to feel about the fact that they were willing to tape themselves, but who was she to judge? He hadn't done anything wrong, and, if she could believe Duke, it was long before she'd met him.

She sighed, hesitated, and then called him.

"*Yo, it's me, you know what to do,*" said his voicemail, followed by a beep.

Angel hung up. She tried twice more over the next half hour, but he didn't answer. She'd started to leave a message once but couldn't get out the words. *I'm sorry,* she wanted to say. *It was me who was not being fair to you. You deserve better.* However, what she'd said at the table, while hurtful, was true. She could not risk Duke getting in her way when she was so close to the finish line. A relationship with so much baggage was out of the question right now.

But he was still a human being. She couldn't leave it this way. He'd been good to Jose. He'd chased her down and apologized when he'd been an ass the night before. He'd been a friend to her. And Angel was just another person who pushed him aside when things got hard. She had to return the favor, swallow her pride, and apologize. She tried calling one last time. No answer.

With a sigh, she gathered up her things and messaged for an Uber.

Chapter Seventeen

There was one car in the drive, a Lexus.

Angel knocked on the front door, praying it was Duke who answered.

It wasn't. The door swung open to reveal a gray-haired gentleman in a sweater vest, with a small gut. A sour, bent version of Duke.

"Hi, I'm sorry to bother you. Is Duke here?" She felt like a child, asking for a friend to come out and play.

The man removed his reading glasses and propped them on his head. "And who are you, miss?"

Here's a guy who doesn't watch the news.

"Um, I met Duke a few days ago . . ."

"Are you the one who spent the night here last night?"

She didn't want to answer. "Yes," she said slowly.

Without another word, he went back inside, leaving the door open. She followed. He still hadn't answered her question about Duke. He waited for her by the table, which was now covered in newspaper and bills, instead of her clothes.

He held out his hand. She went to shake it, but instead of taking her hand, he opened his. Nestled in his palm was Gabriela's gold-and-diamond bracelet.

"This must be yours. It was on the floor in the kitchen when I got home this morning."

Oh, Gabriela. I am a terrible friend. She lifted it from his palm, blushing. "Thank you," she said awkwardly. "Are you Duke's father?"

"Yes. I am Willis Lewis." He moved behind the island and started making coffee.

"I'm Angel. I was at your march for education equality last year. I think it's great what you're doing for the community."

"If only my son felt the same way." He fiddled with the stove.

"So, I take it he's not here?"

Willis took his time before answering. "No. I have no idea where he is."

Well, this is fun. She was about to say thank you to his back and leave, when she noticed a stack of letters on the table next to her. What caught her attention was the looping signature. *Regina.* The letter was handwritten—flowery cursive punctuated by a lot of heavy underlining.

Angel guiltily moved away. Why did Willis have letters from Regina? Or maybe they belonged to Duke? Wasn't his ex out of the picture? What was going on? *Do I really want to know?*

Willis came around the island, putting himself between her and the table, folding his arms across his chest, scowling at her. "I wanted Duke to help organize a luncheon for the aldermen today. As usual, he is not willing to take care of anyone but himself." He narrowed his eyes. "Though he can't even do that right. Believe me, little lady, you're barking up the wrong tree. Duke needs to concentrate and get back in the game. You're going want to find yourself another man to hang on."

Angel took a step back, dismayed. "*Que?*"

"'*Que? Que?*'" the older man mocked. "You know exactly what I'm talking about."

"Mr. Lewis, believe me, I'm not trying to get anything out of Duke." She slung her purse over her shoulder and strode to the kitchen door. "I do think your son could use a real friend. Some support. He's struggling." *Marches for fair treatment, huh?*

He followed. "He has plenty of friends. He doesn't need another woman looking for a meal ticket." With that, the old man opened the door and waved her out.

"You're a real peach, you know that?" she said to him, but he'd already shut the door behind her. She considered pounding on it, making him open up so she could have the last word, but she was too tired. She could see why Duke was glad his father wasn't home the night before.

A car turned into the driveway, startling her.

It was a Bentley, and Kinley was driving.

The reality TV star was as surprised to see Angel as Angel was surprised to see her. But the petite woman quickly got out of the car and approached Angel before she could run away.

Oh God, is she going to take a swing at me?

"Angel, wait. Don't go!" Kinley pleaded. She'd been crying. But, of course, puffiness looked good on her. "I need you to tell me what happened last night."

Angel rounded on her. "You treated me like trash. That's what happened."

"Angel, did you sleep with Roland? Just tell me."

"You can go fuck yourself, Kinley. I've had it with you people!"

"Please, I have to know!"

"For God's sakes, it was Regina."

"I knew it!" The woman wailed, not caring that she was in public, on the street. "I didn't want to believe it."

"She and Roland seem like the perfect couple." Angel instantly regretted her words, as Kinley's forehead tightened and spasmed in pain. "I'm sorry, I shouldn't have said that."

"I know we were horrible to you last night." When Angel didn't respond, Kinley continued, "I mean it. I feel terrible. I just didn't know what to do. My head wasn't right." She swiped at her eye. "I should never have allowed her to do that to a guest in my home."

Angel had no idea what to say. "That's true."

"I'd like to make it up to you. What can I do? Can I take you shopping?"

Angel drew in a sharp breath. "I know you're trying to be nice, but can you hear how condescending that is?"

"No! That's not how I mean it!"

"It's fine. By the way, I left your dress and shoes here. I'm not sure where Duke put them. He's not here." Angel started walking down the sidewalk. "I have to get to the clinic. Thanks for loaning the poor girl an outfit."

Kinley called out from behind her, "At least let me give you a ride. I can get the dress later."

Angel thought about it. She could be stubborn and prideful, or she could let this woman appease her guilt while saving herself a bus ride. She nodded and followed Kinley back to the car.

"The clinic, then? Where's that at?"

"A couple of blocks from the Peacock, in Mount Eden. I can take the bus, really."

"I've got nothing better to do. Duke texted this morning to tell me the dress and shoes were here, so I thought I might as well come get them, give myself a job, do something other than cry."

"I am sorry—"

"Eh." Kinley waved a hand over the steering wheel. "It's not like this is the first time. Roland likes my money so much, you'd think he'd be better at hiding his hookups. But no. Anyway, let's talk about you . . . So. The dress was here this morning, huh?"

Angel buffed her fingernails. She wasn't going to trust Kinley with details.

"Alright. You're not going to talk. Fine. But I want you to know, Duke is a good guy. He might drink too much, or get moody, but in his heart he is truly a good person. If you end up dating, he'd treat you right, if you gave him a chance."

"I'm not sure we're going to be seeing each other again. Things are too complicated."

"Because of last night? I'd assumed he'd made it up to you, if you spent the night . . ."

Angel cut her eyes at the woman. "Haven't you seen the news?"

"You mean today? No. Why?"

She sighed deeply and said through gritted teeth, "A sex tape of Regina and Duke went viral. Duke claims it was from last year."

"You are kidding me!" Kinley's mouth was open. "That bitch. Regina totally leaked it. She has some crazy in her, that one. Listen, I'm sure it really is from last year. I don't think Duke has had anything to do with her since she left him."

"Maybe, maybe not. He's got a stack of letters on his kitchen table right now, from her. His personal life is too messy. I gotta focus on my career right now. I have to. I have to think about my son first."

"I forgot you have a child." Kinley didn't look away from the road, but her mouth puckered.

"Yes," Angel said with an edge. *I will not justify myself—not to her, not to anyone else.*

"I'm just surprised, that's all." Kinley's face deepened in concern. "I guess this does make a difference when it comes to dating."

Now I'm not good enough for Duke?

"Stop with the angsty face, Angel. I'm saying you might be right; Duke may be too messed up for a single mom." Kinsley honked her horn at a car stopped at a green light. "He is a sweetheart, but he's got issues. And I say that with love." She leaned on the horn again. "Come on! Learn to drive! Anyway, are you sure Regina has been writing to him?" She shrugged her slim shoulders. "That's just weird. She tells me she hates him."

Angel leaned her head against the seat rest and closed her eyes. "I saw the letters, signed by her, when I was talking to Duke's father." She opened her eyes again and frowned at Kinley. "Who, by the way, was not very nice."

"Willis? Tell me about it. When Mark was killed last year, it wasn't just Regina who left Duke. Willis treated his son like the shooting was his fault." The beautiful TV star sighed heavily and shook her head. "Duke's had a hard time coming back from not only an injury and loss but the rejection of his friends and family. Roland hasn't been much help, either, that selfish idiot."

They didn't talk much for the remaining few blocks. A heavy gloom sat between them. Kinley handed her a business card as Angel was getting out of the car, apologized again, and told her to call if she ever wanted to talk.

Angel thanked the woman and said good-bye, but by then her mind was a million miles away. Well, really, a hundred feet away, in the office of Dr. Collins. She grimaced, facing the clinic.

Dr. Collins sat down with Angel in his office. His gelled hair was now a startling shade of black. With the black turtleneck sweater, white overcoat, and sallow skin, he resembled a mortician from a B movie.

"We need to reschedule your exit conference. I'm sorry I put it off." He flipped open a desk calendar. "Wouldn't want you to fail the practicum, would we?"

"No, that's true. I'm free today. Right now." It was Wednesday. She only had a few more days to turn in her practicum paperwork to her program director at the school.

"Hmm. Well. You're not really free, are you?"

Angel had no idea what he was talking about. "What do you mean?"

"Darlin'. No need to play it off. Not with me, remember? I was there when you agreed to fake date the Duke."

"Oh, yeah. Right." She shifted in her chair. "But you don't need to worry about me. I'm not trapped into anything."

"I'm not worried. You're a big girl. A smart girl." He rubbed at a smudge on his desk. "I'd recommend staying away from that ballplayer, though. He's not very trustworthy, is he?"

"I don't know about that."

"I do. He has an outstanding bill at the clinic. And he didn't mind taking advantage of you in front of the press, did he, darlin'? Then there's the tape with the model, which must be pretty embarrassing for you, since the press thinks you're his girlfriend."

"I should probably get back to work . . ." Angel wanted desperately to get away from the doctor and the way he drew out every syllable in every word—and the way he inserted himself into her business.

"You know, I've had a number of reporters ask to speak with you. They want to know how you feel about Regina. Should I give them your number?"

"No, I—"

"That's what I thought. A couple have been very persistent, though, wanting information about your personal life. Asking how long you've been dating, where you live, if you have family." The doctor reclined, put his feet up on the desk. "I mean, it would be simply awful if they found out about sweet little Jose. They'd be following him to school, asking him about the Duke. They'd probably ask the child if he knows about the sex tapes . . . They have no shame."

"You haven't said anything, have you?"

"Of course not." He tented his fingers under his chin. "Not yet."

Angel went cold. "What do you mean, 'not yet'?"

He sighed. "This must be trying for you. I can see how revealing Jose's existence, or even the truth about your relationship, would cause a lot of problems for Jose, you, and, yes, obviously the Duke. However, I can be persuaded to stay quiet."

She squinted her eyes at him. *Common decency won't keep you quiet?* "Uh-huh. Keep talking."

He stood up, slowly, and moved around his desk.

He didn't stop until he was behind Angel. "I like you, Angel. I'd like to get to know you better." He was too close, his breath warm on top of her head. He ran his fingertips up her neck, over her bare skin.

Stiffening, she said, "I'm not comfortable with this, Dr. Collins."

His hands dropped to her shoulders and squeezed. "You just need to relax, darlin'. A massage would be good for you."

She tried to stand up. He pressed down, stopping her. "Think about it, Angel. You could really use a friend right now. I could be that friend."

"What are you—"

"I think you know." He swayed back and forth behind her, letting the fly of his pants brush across her back.

It took her half a second to realize exactly what had happened. She leapt up, breaking free from her frozen state of disbelief. "Dr. Collins, please! I'm not interested."

"Ah, I see." He shuffled to the side of his desk. "I want

you to know, I'm here for you. And you can rely on my discretion. If you're here for me." He adjusted his bulging pants. "No need to tell the Duke about this. He's got his own problems."

She swallowed, sour spit filling her throat. "So, to be clear, I either have sex with you or—"

He startled, surprised by her candor. "My dear, no! I would never force you into something you didn't want. The choice is yours. But maybe we should reschedule your exit exam for Friday morning? We both need some time to think about what we're going to say."

With that, he left the room.

Duke stood, his hat twisted in his hands, his head bent in penitence. "Skip, I'm sorry."

The manager sat behind a large black-glass desk, glaring at his pitcher. "Enough with the sorries. I've had it with the sorries. I didn't fly back to New York so I could listen to you whine and simper like a mewling calf. Son, we have asked and asked for you to get it together. I felt bad for you when Mark passed last year, I did . . . But how long do you expect me to put aside good business sense for your fragile ego?"

"I—"

"Shut your fucking mouth, Duke. Unless you're gonna tell me the porno that my kid was watching at the breakfast table was some crazy dream I had, I don't want to hear a goddamn word come out of your mouth."

Duke stayed silent. He felt like crying.

"What can I do? You don't listen to me. You've got an excuse for everything. We're supposed to be a family operation, but our star player is involved in a gang shooting, parties like a goddamn rock star, and, now, is famous for boinking a girl and putting the video on something called YouTube for the children of America to see. The Christian moms are blowing up my email, demanding you be put in jail. And you know what, Duke?" He cocked his head, a fat angry bird. "Despite the hoo-ha and bullshit you've stirred up, I'd find a way to make this work. By God, you've got an arm. How can we afford to lose you?"

Duke heard the "but" coming. Behind the manager, there was a glass wall overlooking Bronx Bolt Stadium. He was afraid this might be the last time he was here as a player.

"But I think you're lying about your injury," Skip said. "That's a deal breaker for me. Are you healed or not?"

"I was at that clinic to see Angel, the nurse . . ."

"You did not answer my question."

"Listen, Skip, I can prove I'm fine."

"That's right, you will. I'll have the team doctor and a hitter here the day after tomorrow, and you're going to pitch for me." The manager stood up. "This is a team. If you can't be one hundred fucking percent, for your team, then you gotta step aside. Alright. Get out."

Duke's hand on the doorknob, the manager stopped him, saying, "If the newspapers or TV or any goddamn media so much as whispers your name for any reason, don't bother showing up on Friday."

"Mama?"

"Hmm?"

"Mama, will you read to me?"

"Hmm?"

"Mama! You said—"

"Baby! Please! Can you just go to bed?"

Jose's bottom lip quivered as he stomped past her to his room. He slammed his door.

Angel shoved a pencil into her hair and sighed. *Mom of the year, right here.*

There was a knock on the front door. She almost screamed in frustration.

On the other side of the peephole was Aaron. Duke's agent. *Seriously, are you kidding me right now?*

"What do you want?" she yelled, without opening the door.

"You're not going to open up? Classy, Angel." His voice was muffled.

She ripped open the door. "Oh, I'm the one who needs to worry about being classy? Give me a break. Bribing a doctor—"

"Shh! Jesus!" Aaron stepped closer to her.

She held her ground. "Nah, you're not coming in. What do you want?"

"Willis said you left this behind." He reached into the

pocket of his hipster jeans and then dangled a gold brace-let from his squat fingers. Gabriela's bracelet. Angel must have left it on Duke's kitchen table, a second time. Her friend's family heirloom.

"Thanks."

"So. What else did you leave there?" Aaron checked his cuff links. "You got something else you think you need to go get?"

"Huh?" Her confusion was over in a flash. "You think I planted that bracelet?"

"Oh. No. Not you. You not lookin' for a sugar daddy, right, Angel?"

Angel forced a laugh. "I mean . . . Wow. What, you afraid I might steal your sugar?" Before he could answer, she continued, "Dude, I am not interested in your man. We've parted ways."

"Wait." The agent furrowed his brow. "He's not here?"

Chapter Eighteen

Angel dreamed of falling. She'd been on the edge of a roof—the clinic's roof, but in the dream it commanded a view of her college campus. Dr. Collins stood to one side of her, Duke on the other. They were shouting at each other, so she'd jumped. She fell, and fell, and fell. The fall was infinite. She had no control and no idea of how or when it was going to end. Afraid and frustrated, she screamed.

She woke, the scream pressing against her closed lips—a long, muffled moan in real life. She kicked the blankets off and the air cooled her sweaty skin. She cringed away from the bright red lights on the alarm clock. Angel squeezed her eyes shut again, but it was no better, her mind free-falling back into a dream state, the same dream on reset.

Groggy, she forced herself from the bed. It was an hour

before her alarm was set to go off. Just one more thing the idiot men in her life had stolen from her. Dignity, peace, and now sleep.

The steam tendrils from her cup of coffee caressed her face. She contemplated the small apartment around her. *Jose and I are fine here, as we are. I mean, sure, less mold would be nice, but we don't need riches and a crazy lifestyle. We do, however, need a roof over our heads.* Angel's stomach squeezed at the decision before her. She needed to pass her exams so she could get a permanent nursing job, but Dr. Collins . . . She shuddered. The thought of his fingers touching her, groping her. Bile rose in her throat. She couldn't do it. She was going to lose a career before she really got started.

Pft. She leaned back in the chair, forced herself to stretch out the tenseness. *We will be fine, too. I don't have to be a nurse. I'm a hard worker. I can bartend . . . Okay, not at the Peacock, but somewhere. Hell, I can join the army.*

But how would she buy Jose's medicine between jobs? Or pay rent? It was all so complicated. Her head throbbed. *Enough of that. I will focus on what I can do, right now. I'll worry about later . . . later.*

Maybe the doctor was bluffing.

Randomly, her eyes settled on a dish towel on the counter and, suddenly, thoughts of the doctor and what was surely a wormy penis faded to number two on the worry list as she remembered the pile of bathroom towels she'd forgotten to wash. Shit. Jose was going to have to use one of her T-shirts to dry off after his shower. Again.

•   •   •

The early rays of dawn filtered under the blinds in Duke's bedroom. He lay on his back in bed, unable to appreciate the high thread count of his sheets or the rough-hewn cedar ceiling beams he'd been staring at for hours.

He'd spent the afternoon and evening before in his car, staring at dark, choppy waves in Long Island Sound, ignoring his phone and drinking beer as his brain looped over and over what was said at the meeting with his manager. Staring had yet to solve his problem.

Choice one: admit my ankle isn't healed, become a loser.

Choice two: get the crazy doctor to shoot me up with steroids and painkillers, lie my ass off.

I just wanted to be a good guy and play ball. What happened? He could see why Angel steered clear of him. He wouldn't drag her back in.

The morning light was moving over the walls, getting stronger. Duke heaved himself out of bed, threw on a pair of shorts, and made his way to his dad's side of the house. Knocking on the suite door, he said, "Pops? Pops, I need to talk to you."

After a second, the door cracked open. Willis, eyes heavy with sleep, wore a short silk bathrobe. "Now?"

"What are you wear—" Duke bit his tongue. "Sorry. I know it's early."

The old man rubbed his eyes. "You fired me, remember? I'm going back to bed."

"We have to deal with this shit that's goin' down. I need your help."

"This is new. You asking me for anything. I texted you two nights ago."

"Please."

Willis sighed. "I'll meet you downstairs. Make the coffee."

"I paid for your first visit, but not the second, not yet." Willis dropped three cubes of sugar into his mug and stirred with vigor. "I told that charlatan I'd get him the rest of his money after I talked to you—which I thought would be yesterday. You ignored my texts."

"Yeah." Duke was tired. If he was to be honest with himself, he was also scared. "Anyway, I think I'm going to have to see him again today, which means more money."

His pops made a strange gurgling noise and set down the spoon. "First things first. Why do you have to go back?"

"Skip says I have to report to the stadium tomorrow. A team doctor will be there, and I'm supposed to show I have stamina on the mound. I have to prove I'm healed."

"So? You told me you were. Why do you need this clinic guy again?" Willis's eyebrows knitted together. "Are you about to do something stupid?"

"That's why I wanted to talk to you! I don't know what to do!" Duke felt the panic cresting, about to overwhelm him. He took a breath. "My ankle is not healed, alright? It was sore after the charity game, but then I tweaked it play-ing ball with some kids. I'm thinking I'm gonna have to let the doctor give me a shot of something, so I can make it through this thing tomorrow."

"Son—" Willis cut himself off. "Maybe we do need to talk about the money now. It might have bearing on your choices."

"Oh, Jesus."

"You have no money, Duke. If you don't play baseball this season, we will have nothing."

Duke exploded. "Are you kidding me?"

"Okay, slow down. There's more you need to know."

Duke pounded on the table. "I have nothing? *Nothing?* How could you let this happen?"

"That's what I need to tell you. But you have to calm down."

"What'd ya do with my fucking money, old man?"

"It's Regina. She has a video she recorded on her phone. At the bar in Chicago. Footage of you shooting Mark."

The air left the room.

"I did not kill Mark." Duke ground out each word.

"I've got your back, son, I do, but I saw the video."

"I don't know what you saw, but you're wrong. If you think I could do this thing, you do *not* have my back."

"If Regina hadn't shown me the video, I would never believe it, Duke. But I saw you. I cannot unsee it. And I can't let her hurt you. That's where your money has gone."

"This is crazy! She's blackmailing you? Is that what you mean?"

"Yes. She keeps coming back and asking for more money. What am I supposed to do? Let you go to prison?"

"I am not a murderer! Show me the video."

"Regina has it, but I do have a copy on a flash drive. At the bank, in a lockbox. I can get it today."

"How much has she suckered you for, Pops?"

"I'd say she's been paid close to ten million. And now . . . now she's asking for another fifteen."

"No. No. No! This is just unbelievable!"

"On top of the massive legal fees, medical bills, and partying . . . we're wiped out. We gonna have to sell the house."

"I can't handle this. It's too much." He had no words, no ability to plan, no route to dodge and weave. Regina. Releasing the sex video—which he desperately regretted making in the first place—and now a falsified video of the shooting? Why would she hate Duke so much, do this to him? She'd left him, not the other way around.

He stood and paced. Finally he stopped, placed both hands flat on the bar to hold himself up. His head hung in defeat. "I guess I have to go back to the quack at the clinic. What choice do I have? If I don't get a steroid shot in my ankle before the pitching test, I'll lose my job. And the house, I guess. Then what do we do? Sleep in the car? Or is that about to be taken away, too?"

"Listen, we'll find a way. Sit down, son."

Duke went back to pacing instead. "No matter what, Pops, I'm going to prove to you Regina has made some fake-ass video. I am getting that money back."

"I believe you, okay? I'm sorry—I thought I was doing the right thing. But even if we can prove the recording is fake, as soon as you go after her, you got another scandal on your hands. We have to think this through. Carefully."

"Okay. I'll put the backstabbing bitch on the back burner, but just until I get through pitching tomorrow."

"Right. One thing at a time. What's your first move, you think?"

"I'm gonna have to get money for the doc." Duke stopped pacing. "Maybe Roland will help. He fucking owes me."

"Why's that?"

Duke sighed. "Later, Pops."

Angel tried handing Jose a sack lunch as he put his school stuff in his Pokémon backpack. He put his hands on his hips. "Mom, it's Thursday."

"Yeah? What's that matter?"

"I told you! You signed the permission slip!"

"Um, yes, of course . . ." She had no idea what he was talking about.

Jose rolled his eyes, a small, irritated man. "I mean,

seriously, Mom. Our class is going to watch The King and I. That play? Remember?"

"Ah, okay, it's coming back to me. Mrs. Jones has lunches for you. Right?"

Jose huffed around the living room.

She dropped Jose's lunch sack on the counter. She'd used the rest of the bread to make him a peanut butter sandwich—now she'd have something to eat for breakfast. Not that she was hungry. Her stomach was full of stress knots. Was it about work? Or the Duke? The King and I . . . *Isn't that about the nanny and that king? And he's a jerk? . . . Huh. Life is funny.*

She walked Jose to his elementary school and then returned home to study for an hour before she reported to work at the dreaded clinic. Gabriela called out a hello from the salon, the woman's hair and makeup fully done, a vision in a pink jumpsuit, set off by a pink stripe in her long black hair.

"You look pretty," Angel said with a small wave. "Why you here so early?"

Gabriela shrugged, held up an armful of dirty towels. "No one else is gonna do it. Did you get ahold of Duke last night? Such a shame, the two of you not talking when you just finally got laid."

"Leave it to you to remind me about my sex life. And dirty towels." Angel followed Gabriela around the room as the hairdresser retrieved supplies. "Hey, I have your stole and bracelet. I shoulda given them to you yesterday, I'm sorry. I can get them right now. And maybe I could throw a couple of towels in with your load? I'm failing at the whole adulting thing lately, big-time."

"No worries. I'll pick up my stuff later, and your towels, after Jose gets home. I'm picking him up today, right?"

"Yeah, I'm at the clinic for a twelve-hour shift. I hope you know how much I appreciate all you do, Gabriela. I really do. You're such a good friend."

"Sugar, we family. We do family." She gave Angel a hug. "My sister from another motha, I know everything seems hard and impossible right now, but things will be so much better when you get your degree and you have a steady job. You'll see. You're almost there."

As Angel squeezed the older woman back, she let herself melt into the embrace for a moment, soaking in the unconditional love of a true friend. She almost told Gabriela about Dr. Collins's ultimatums, but then straightened, pulled away, and blocked off her swirling emotions. No need to burden Gabriela. There was nothing she could do anyway.

Upstairs, she chewed the tasteless peanut butter sandwich, flipping through a textbook listlessly. *I know I shouldn't, but I miss Duke. I told him to leave me alone . . . Why did he have to listen to me?* She got up and retrieved Gabriela's things, putting the wrap on the couch, laying the gold-and-diamond bracelet across the lovely white fur. Gabriela would see them later. And Angel could glance at them as she studied. A lot had happened the night she'd dressed up and attended the party, so much of it exciting and wonderful. Would she go back if she could?

No, I don't belong in that world. I can't pretend I'm royalty. And I don't want to.

Angel arrived at work, nervous tension bringing her shoulders up to her ears. No matter how many deep breaths she slowly exhaled or fields of flowers she pictured, she couldn't relax. But after a suspiciously pleasant few hours, she started to second-guess herself.

Dr. Collins was polite, even normal, assigning her reasonable tasks, acting as if nothing had happened. *Maybe I'm remembering the conversation wrong. Was I being a drama queen?*

Halfway through her shift, she felt a text notification vibrate from the phone in her pocket. On her break, she found a message from Duke. It was not what she expected. Actually, she hadn't expected anything.

> *I know you don't want to talk to me, but I need to see the doc right away. Today. It's an emergency. Do you think you could sneak me in the back? Last favor I'll ask, I promise.*

Low levels of anger rippled through Angel. He didn't respond to any of her messages after she graciously tried to apologize for blowing him off, despite the fact that she'd spent the night with him and then saw him having sex with Regina . . . Now he wanted a favor? It boggled her mind. She fought cynicism, but it won.

When exactly did you realize how handy it is to have a nurse under your belt?

There was a full moment before he responded.

I did not bring you home just so I could use you. But I can see why'd you think that and I'm sorry. I really did like you.

He said *did like*, past tense. That was disappointing, in a confusing sort of way. Then he sent another text.

Angel, please, we need to talk. But getting to Collins is a matter of life and death. Can you open the back door, 5 minutes?

She'd at least get to see him, to clear her conscience and apologize to Duke for not letting him speak his side yesterday.

Okay, fine. Btw, Dr. Collins is obsessed with you paying your bill.

Angel had no idea what was going on. He was a famous ballplayer. Why wouldn't Duke pay him, get it out of the way? It was odd enough that Duke was trying to hide his medical visits—which she only half agreed with—but why give the doctor so much leverage? It had to be exhausting to live life under the shadow of being caught in a lie.

She refused to carry that thought any further, afraid it might lead to self-analysis.

She was heading down the back hallway when Theresa caught up with her. "Whatcha doin'? Ms. Rodriguez is waiting for you. And, um, I'm sorry, she needs her toenails cut again."

Angel sighed. "If I ever get that heavy and can't cut my own toenails, please, just shoot me."

"I feel sorry for her," Theresa said.

"Yeah, me too. Until I have to saw through her yellow goat hooves."

Angel again found herself wanting to confide in a friend, this time the other student nurse. It would be a relief to share her burden, to ask advice about the weird situation. But no. It was bad enough that she was allowing herself to be roped back into this stupid charade, she couldn't bring her friends into her problems.

I'm letting Duke in, then he's on his own.

"I'll be there in a second," she said to Theresa. She couldn't come up with any reason why she'd be heading out the back door, so she didn't bother explaining. She heard the girl jog toward the exam rooms, going back to her patients, as Angel should be doing.

She used her badge to turn off the door alarm. She was surprised to find Willis, not Duke, sitting on the back stoop. Before she could say anything, the older man stood up and jerked a thumb over his shoulder. Peering down the narrow alley, she spied a guy with a hoodie drawn tight over his head, crouched behind a Dumpster. Her stomach dropped. Something was terribly wrong if this was a successful ballplayer, stooping to such lows.

"Hey," Duke's father said at her in a low hiss. "Is anyone else around?"

She refused to whisper. "You're clear." Louder, she said, "Get in here already." She held the door as Willis and then Duke shuffled through the back entrance. Without a word, Willis strode a few steps ahead of them, as if he were in charge. Duke, meanwhile, repeatedly peeked behind him. Checking for witnesses, she guessed.

"You look completely crazy, you know."

"I might be." His green eyes lit on her, wide and alert. "Angel, does Dr. Collins know I'm here?"

"No. I figured I'd get you into an exam room first. I didn't want to give him time to stew. Or do anything stupid."

Willis made no comment to either of them, only pushed open the door to the first room they came to. It was an exam room they used for storage. He regarded with disdain the stacks of boxes containing paper towels, toilet paper, and piles of extra blankets, as if he were surrounded by dirty diapers. "How 'bout if we wait in here?"

Duke moved into the dark room, keeping his hood on. But he reached out and lightly touched Angel on the arm.

"Thanks. I don't know what I'd do without you . . . being here. You have no idea."

She wanted to fall into him, embrace him with her entire body pressed against his. The memory of their closeness was too fresh, too tantalizing. "I'll go find Dr. Collins."

Duke's father dropped the blinds on the window into the hall and flipped on the light. His skin appeared sallow and his gray curls had yellow highlights under the harsh fluorescent light. To her, he said coldly, "Girl, you best keep your mouth shut if anyone asks you questions."

"How about if I take a swing at your head instead?" Angel growled at him. "The crap I put up with because of you two—"

"Pops! You don't know nothin'. This here girl has stood with me from the start, and she don't even know me. She ain't blood."

Angel was thrilled to be defended in such a way, but Willis nodded sarcastically. "Uh-huh. I hear ya. Take digs all you want, but I am blood, whether you like it or not, and that's not goin' away." He turned to Angel. "Why you still here?"

Glaring at him, she slammed the door. Their bickering was audible. *I am so lucky my mama was a decent human being.*

She found Dr. Collins in his office. "Can I interrupt for a minute?"

"Ah. So you've changed your mind. Smart girl. Shut the door."

She gulped, dismay trying to take over her senses. Dr. Collins had not been bluffing yesterday, then. "It's about Duke. He's in exam six. He and his dad are waiting to see you."

He straightened his long lab coat, a satisfied smile on his face. "Finally. He's paying up, darlin'." The doctor chucked her under the chin as he moved past. "As good little boys and girls do, if they don't want to get in trouble."

She backpedaled, just barely restraining herself—she'd almost slapped him. Putting as much distance between them as she could, she gave herself a stern lecture. *Now is not the time to give in to violent impulses. That got you fired from the bar, remember?*

Part of her wanted to see Willis and Dr. Collins in the same room together. The doctor, who tried to come off as a slick southern good ol' boy, and the financial manager, who was arrogant and snide. Two alpha dogs fighting over the bone that was Duke's money. But the smarter, bigger part of her wanted to get on with her job and let them get on with their sideways business behind closed doors.

After a second's hesitation, she chose to clip the gnarled toenails of the cranky old diabetic lady in exam three instead of going to Duke.

"You've got quite the brass pair, comin' in and askin' for more favors. Y'all like to write checks with your mouths you don't seem to be able to cash."

"I can pay." Duke hated himself for the note of pleading he heard in his own voice. Desperation leaked out as body odor from his pores, making him grateful Angel was not there to smell his sour weakness. She already thought he was a disgusting human, no need to reinforce it.

"Yes? Let's see it." The doctor abruptly lost his heavy southern drawl, overcome by greed.

Willis made a disgusted noise and opened the briefcase, revealing stacks of cash.

The doctor's face did not change, but his body quivered, tight as a guitar string, ready to shiver or snap, depending on the next move in the room. He picked up a stack held together with rubber bands, thumbing through it. "How much is here?"

Duke's father took the bundle back from the doctor, replaced it, then closed the briefcase. "There's enough to pay the past due bills, and enough to cover the cost of the procedure you're about to perform." Then he handed him a form. "This is a nondisclosure agreement. Sign it and we'll make it worth your while."

This is where Pops shines: organization and graft.

"I'm intrigued." Dr. Collins fingered his turtleneck for a second.

With his overly black pompadour and horsey face, he might have been an bad actor in a hemorrhoids commercial. Standing next to Willis, who easily pulled off the community leader persona—regal in his dress shirt and slacks, his gray curls clipped and professional, his posture straight and easy—the doctor appeared foolish. Duke was relieved when Collins signed the paper and seemed to regain his composure. And his accent.

"What is it you boys have in mind?"

Duke shoved aside a pile of towels that were being stored on an exam table and hopped up, his leg stretched in front of him. "Look here, Doc, my ankle is worse. Tomorrow I have to stand and pitch in front of a team doctor and my manager. I'm afraid I'll buckle. Unless you can give me something so I don't feel the pain, something that won't be detected in a drug test."

"Hmm. You're willing to do this so you can pitch for one day? What happens next week, when you're supposed to be back to pitching full-time? Your ankle won't be a hundred percent in seven days. There will not be a miracle healing here. Frankly, this stunt may wreck you for the season if you're not careful."

"What do you care? I'll cross that bridge when I come to it. I wanna get through tomorrow. Can you do it? Can you help me?"

"I'll have to check my drug room, make sure I have the right supplies. I'll be back—"

Duke cringed when his father grabbed the doctor's arm. He felt like a little kid, watching a parent about to get in a fight with the principal. He remained mute, however, as Willis said, "Uh-huh. I'll come with you. So's you don't make any calls."

"Hmph. You're not dealing with a hooligan. I stick to my word. Besides, I signed your little form."

The doctor pushed his way out. Willis stubbornly followed.

Suddenly alone in a quiet, cramped room, Duke glowered at his ankle. It looked fine. It wasn't even swollen. *Am I sure this is what I wanna do? I could just tell the truth.* He went back and forth in his head but was repeatedly blocked by the knowledge that if he took the high road and walked out without dampening the pain, he risked losing his job tomorrow, and his house and his lifestyle and his career prospects soon thereafter. He was trapped.

The two men returned. The doctor handed him a vial and a syringe. "Your father can administer the shot directly in your ankle"—he touched a spot behind the knob on Duke's ankle—"the morning of your meeting. It's similar to a steroid but undetectable." The gaunt man removed a prescription bottle from his pocket. "This is a painkiller that should numb the residual pain without making you woozy—though no promises. Everyone reacts differently. However, it is acetaminophen-based, so it won't show up on a tox screen." He scratched his head. "Hmm. Well, heavy usage can create a false positive for cannabis, but that's a very slim chance. Don't use it until tomorrow. It won't have time to build up in your liver."

A blinding headache crashed over Duke, paralyzing his thoughts. He paled.

Willis nodded to his son, misreading his response. He said, "I can do it. No worries." His father was so sure of himself, like for him there was no other course of action. The assurances of a gambler and a cheat didn't quell Duke's doubts, however.

After the doctor escorted them outside, via the back doors, Duke and Willis found Roland and Aaron waiting at the end of the alley, anonymous behind the tinted windows of an SUV. As father and son ducked into the back, Roland twisted in the passenger seat, appraising Duke. "So?" The retired player asked. "Does it feel better? You good, bro?"

Duke refused to meet his eyes. "Let's just go."

"Where am I taking you? Home?" his agent asked, anxiety in his voice.

No one answered him.

Chapter Nineteen

Angel was refilling glove and sanitary lotion stations when she saw the doctor drift down the hall, toward the back doors, holding a briefcase. Trying to stop herself, she peeked into Duke's room, only to find it empty. He had not stopped to say good-bye.

Typical male. Got what he needed and left. So glad I could be here for him.

Terrified of what was expected of her the next day, she wanted to leave, too, and never come back. But she was going to have to pull up her big-girl panties and face the doctor sometime.

I want to keep my panties on, though, she thought miserably. She had a choice, sure, but it wasn't a good one.

She was sitting at the nurse's station, filling out paperwork, when her pager went off. It was Dr. Collins. She was to be at his office at nine a.m. the next day.

A few hours later, Angel begged Theresa to cover her. The doctor was gone, but her stomach would not quit rolling. When her feet hit the sidewalk outside, she almost cried in relief.

Her final exams were to start on Monday, assuming she made it through tomorrow. If Dr. Collins didn't sign off on her practicum, she would not have to worry about next week. She'd have failed the program. And if the doctor was provoked enough to fail her, he'd probably also give the press the real details about her and Duke—and Jose.

Twenty minutes later, she opened the door to House of Beauty, intent on closing herself up in her apartment. The salon was quiet, only Latisha and Gabriela working. Latisha was in the back, giving an elderly blind woman from the neighborhood a perm and telling her racy stories about the people on the block.

The only other customer was in Gabriela's chair.

"*Valgame Dios!*" Angel blinked, to be sure her tired eyes hadn't given up. "Oh my God," she repeated. "What are you doing here?"

Duke sat with a black apron tented over his long body, his green eyes shining under the lights, not dimmed by a hat brim. Gabriela trimmed his curls, moving her hands as if handling spun glass.

"Angel." He started to stand, but Gabriela put a hand on his chest and pushed him back.

"Nuh-uh." The hairdresser flicked his ear. "Not until

I'm done. She can talk to you over here. We ain't got no secrets, right, baby girl?"

Duke held his ear. "Ow. That hurt."

I wish there were no secrets. Wouldn't it be nice if Duke and I could just lay it all out, right here. "Don't worry about her, Duke. She knows what's up. She's not saying anything." Angel tentatively sat in the next chair, off balance. Unsure of what to do next. A constant state of mind these days.

"I'm sure you deserved it," Gabriela said to Duke. She pumped some product onto her palms and ran it through his hair, pleasure puckering her lips. "So, tell Angel why you're here."

"I'm not sure I want to know," the student nurse said quietly. "Unless it's to apologize."

"I do apologize. Again." Then Duke hissed, Gabriela twisting his ear sharply. "What? I wasn't being sarcastic. The situation has been unfair to you, Angel."

"Yep." Angel tried to keep going, to follow it up with her own apology, the one she'd been trying to give him since yesterday, when she hadn't given him any grace, but she wasn't feeling it anymore.

"Will you go to dinner with me tonight?"

"Why?"

"Okay, fair question." Guilt crept across his face. "The clubhouse is still watchin'. It would really help if you could continue pretending to be interested in me, just for tonight. Besides, the least I could do is buy you a nice dinner."

"While letting paparazzi take pictures of me chewing my food, or trying to get a crotch shot as I climb out of a car? Maybe ask me for a review of the sex tape."

"I'll get Aaron to come along, to control the press."

"Oh, good. If he's going, count me in. He's a ball of fun, that one."

"He doesn't have to sit with us. I wouldn't want him to, anyway," he said. Angel saw him dart his eyes at Gabriela's image in the mirror. The hairdresser intently followed the conversation, lightly holding on to his ear. Angel grinned at her. Duke continued, carefully, "I'd like to work some things out. I don't want to have dinner just for a photo op."

"Uh-huh. I'm sure." What was he after? Did he really want to see her or was she the easiest way to solve a problem? She wasn't about to make her heart vulnerable again, even for this handsome, charming man. His energy drew her in every time, and her brain refused to stop the slide show from the culminating moments of their last date— the skin on his dusky chest, slick with sweat under her palms; his lusty groans vibrating against her shoulder; his smell, like the earth after a rain; the salty, ocean-tinged taste of him. He pleased every one of her senses. He'd pleased her multiple times.

"I know you have no reason to say yes. But what if we call it a meeting. No strings attached. Two friends eating together? Anywhere you want. We can even go in to the city."

"Anywhere?"

"Yes. Absolutely."

"Alright," she said thoughtfully, propping her chin with her fist. Something had just occurred to her. "Then I'm gonna get something out of it, *hermano*. Let's go to the Peacock. Frank said if I brought you back in and talked you into getting your picture taken with him, he'd let me have my job back. After tomorrow, I'm probably going to need it."

Both Gabriela and Duke looked at her sharply.

"Girl, what you talkin' about?" Gabriela asked. "You too good for that place. You'll get a nursing job, easy peasy."

"Mmm." Angel hadn't meant to say that aloud. "You know. Tomorrow is my exit interview. Not sure if I'm going to pass my practicum or not."

"Oh, please. You bust your ass for that clinic." Gabriela turned back to Duke, running her fingers through his hair again. She was done, but she clearly didn't want to stop touching him.

Angel forced a small laugh. "Ha. I know. I worry too much."

Duke hadn't said anything, but he was watching her. She hoped he wouldn't ask about Dr. Collins directly; she didn't know if she could keep the man's threats to herself.

Instead, he said, "The Peacock it is."

Gabriela squinted at Angel, butting in. "Are you sure?

You don't need to do this. Not any of it." She dug her fingers into Duke's scalp, making him wince before she released him. "Jose will be done with practice soon. I'll go get him. If that's what you want, Angel, you two go ahead."

"I can't stay long." Angel hadn't meant this minute. It was early for dinner. She glanced at Duke. "Why don't you go ahead? I'll meet you there in thirty minutes." She flipped a hand over her scrubs. "I couldn't care less what anyone at the Peacock thinks, but I don't want your photographers immortalizing me with smeared mascara and stained scrubs, looking like I just ran a marathon."

"A triathlon, really," Gabriela said.

"Why are we friends, again?"

Gabriela blew a kiss at her, then slipped the black drape off of Duke. "Alright. You're done. I'll walk out with you, Duke," the hairdresser said sternly. "Latisha," she called out, "lock the door if you leave." Then she waved her phone at Angel. "Call me if you need me. I wouldn't mind beatin' some ass." This last was said with a head toss and a smile toward Duke.

"Oh. It's you," said the hostess at the door of the Peacock. Her breath hung on the air between them, laced with frost.

The young woman didn't have the decency to blush, though Angel did. The last time she'd seen her, the girl had been exercising her right to fuck her way up the ladder. Now, her eyes blank, the hostess said, "Someone is waiting for you by the bar." Then she zoned completely out, twitching her stiff blond hair and staring over Angel's shoulder.

Angel rolled her eyes. It wasn't easy, deciding not to take her anxiety and ever-present anger out on the rude young woman, but Angel didn't want to waste a burst of energy on a nonentity. She wanted her senses keen and alert.

She wound her way through the tables, surrounded by the night's first wave of club patrons—the men with their ties loosened but on, many of the women still in their workday ballet flats, and the black linen tablecloths already covered with wine bottles, martini glasses, and cheese boards. The DJ was warming up the crowd with old-school rap mash-ups, including Run DMC and Vanilla Ice.

"Angel-l-l," crooned Frank. He hovered over Duke, who sat in the center of a cluster of overstuffed chairs, his feet up on a coffee table. The Bronx Bolt pitcher was on a low-lit dais in the middle of the club, highly visible to patrons, the owner fluttering around him. Everyone in the place would know that a famous professional athlete was in the house.

"Sooo glad to see you again. We've missed you around here." As Frank focused on Angel at the foot of the stairs, his eyes were more bloodshot than usual, highlighted by a tequila sunrise tan. "Come by next week if you're interested in getting back on the schedule."

"Uh, sure, Frank. I'll do that." *I hope to God I don't have to work with this troll again.* The one upside, though, was that the owner of the Peacock was a wimp, easy to manipulate. Dr. Collins was a nightmare with too much power over her. The Peacock might not be so bad . . .

"Frank, is it?" Duke rumbled. "I'll find you later. I hear you want a picture."

"I would be honored if—"

"Okay. My agent's over there. Set it up with him." Duke then shifted his attention to Angel, pointedly ignoring Frank until he bumbled his way off the dais. "I'm surprised Gabriela didn't come with you, to protect you from the big, bad man." He unfolded his lanky body and held out a hand, helping her up the three steps to the platform. She liked the courtliness of the gesture, considering the flimsy nature of the black heels she'd changed into. She was also pleased he wasn't hiding behind a baseball cap, even if it was so he could offer up his face to the press. Her heart tripped when his green eyes crinkled in a smile.

"I forgot to ask earlier, how's the studying? How are you? Besides being mad at me, of course."

"I'm fine." *Dr. Collins is going to stop giving me Jose's medicine, fail me at my practicum, and tell the press where I live if I don't have sex with him tomorrow, but, yeah, I'm fine.* "I'm not really mad at you, you know. I shouldn't have been so harsh, pushed you away like that. I tried to find you yesterday, to tell you I understand the video wasn't your fault."

"I saw your texts. But I could also see you wanted to

separate yourself from my crazy. I get that," he said lightly. Then he let his glance travel down her body. "You look beautiful, by the way."

"And I didn't even borrow this." She plucked at the little black dress she'd dug out of the back of her closet. There were worn shiny patches, thanks to years of use, but it clung to her curves in the right places, and the color fade didn't show in the dim light. Before he could respond, she said, "Gabriela is only making sure I don't get hurt. She's a good friend."

"I wouldn't know. I don't think I have any of those left." He watched her sink into a chair before also sitting back down, candlelight playing off his smooth mahogany skin and square jaw. And his eyes. Those amazing, translucent eyes.

She shook herself free from his spell. "Feel sorry for yourself much?"

"Eh, come on, Angel. You know some of what I'm going through, but not everything."

"While we wait for the vultures to descend, maybe you can fill me in. Start with what happened at the doctor's today, why it was so important you were there."

"Just so you know, two or three vultures have already landed. Aaron is keeping 'em busy at the bar, promising photo ops when we're done eating, but only if they give us space to enjoy our 'date.' But he's not quite as cool about it . . . I think he's trying to videotape us." When Duke pointed directly at Frank, who was trying to hide behind a post, the club owner pretended to answer a call and trotted away. The ballplayer's lips lifted in amusement, but then the look faded as he spoke.

"I can't thank you enough for helping me get in to see Collins today. My manager doesn't believe I'm feeling okay, so he's making me pitch in front of him tomorrow, at the stadium. The problem is, I'm having trouble walking straight, so there's no chance I can stand on a mound and pitch more than once or twice before it's obvious I'm favoring my ankle."

His hand was gripping the armrest between them; she laid her hand sympathetically on his. Friends could touch friends, right? "I'm afraid to ask, but what did you have the doctor do?"

"He gave me medication to dull the pain in my ankle for tomorrow."

She removed her hand. "You're not serious? You're going to end up hurting yourself permanently! Not to mention, you'll have to keep this crazy facade going. Duke, you need to tell your manager the truth."

"There's more to this than just my ego." He handed her the drink menu. "It gets complicated. You're going to want a drink."

"I don't need the menu, I've got it memorized. Tell me what's going on."

"I want a drink first."

"I think you should try club soda for once. Sounds like you need to stay on top of things right now."

Duke's face drained of emotion. He scanned the people at the bar. "Where's Aaron? Maybe we get pics now and get out of here."

"You're right, you're right. I didn't mean to sound judgy." She tucked her hair behind her ear and motioned for one of the servers to take their order. That done, Angel said, "What's so complicated?"

Over the next five minutes, Duke blew her mind. She'd thought her future looked bleak.

As he spoke, she scooted her chair closer and closer, moving in to hear him better over the club's music. His words came low and quick, his eyes glued on his drink. Sometimes his voice would break, just for a second, as he explained how Regina claimed to have a recording of him shooting Mark and that she'd blackmailed his father for millions, to keep him quiet.

I guess I can relax about those letters on Willis's table, she thought, but she didn't feel any more settled than before.

"Now, my savings is gone. Poof. To get the steroids or whatever for my ankle, I had to borrow money from Roland."

"Wait a minute. You're talking to him? You borrowed money from that guy?"

"Yeah, well, I might not like what he did to his wife, and that he did it with Regina, of all people . . . I mean, yeah, he's not always a good person. But he's not going to rat me out for going to the doc, and he has the money. Until Kinley takes it from him, anyway."

"Duke, why use the drugs? You can stop this."

A number of emotions coiled across his face. "If I don't numb my ankle, it will put a stop to everything. Including my career, which I love, but it's also my only way to make money and keep Regina off my back."

"Jeez, there is so much to unpack here." She considered telling him about the doctor's threats to her and how she might be revealed as his fake girlfriend, despite this new round of photos of them together, but he didn't seem like he could take one more bit of bad news. *God, I hope I can find a way to protect both of us tomorrow.* She refocused on the conversation at hand. "Regina wants more money? You're talking like the video she has is real, that it can implicate you for murder. If it's not real, you don't have to pay her. As a matter of fact, you can have that bitch arrested for extortion."

"I'm not willing to risk it."

"The video . . ."

"Yes?"

"Does it make you look bad, Duke? Is that it?"

"I need time to prove she's a fraud! Jesus! You're no different than my father." He sat up straight, leaning away from her. "Worse, even. He's never pretended to believe in me. You . . ."

"Duke—"

Aaron materialized between them. "What's going on, kids?" He smiled, a shark smile, and, without moving his lips, said, "You two better get your shit together. Let the reporters take their pictures and then you can argue. Somewhere else."

Duke folded his arms. "I don't think they're lip-readers. I can barely hear myself over this music."

"Then maybe smile and stop throwing your hands around."

"Aaron," Angel said, "why don't you go away?" There were so many people pulling the strings around her, trying to control both her and Duke, she couldn't take one more tug. When Aaron didn't move, she said, "You want a real scene, agent boy? Move along."

"I don't know what you have against me." He put a protective hand between them, but Duke gave him a head nod, gesturing toward the bar.

Muttering, but with a smile on his face, he went away.

Angel bent close to Duke as he slumped into the chair, miserable. Her voice soft, she said, "I wish life was easier, Duke. And I do believe in you. But I still think the only way you're going to have peace in your life, or be able to find any joy in your days, is if you stop hiding stuff. You can't live a lie. It'll kill you." She grimaced. If only she would take her own advice.

Duke stood up. "Angel, enough. You don't understand. I'm doing this. I have to." He held his hand out to her. "Are you still willing to get your picture taken with me? I'd like to get this over with."

This conversation? This date? What did he want over? In the beginning, she'd helped him because he was decent to

Jose. Then she stuck with him because he'd made her feel special and wanted, for far too short a time. She didn't ask for clarification, simply followed him down the stairs, a tight, fake smile on her face. She could front with the best of them. As Aaron and Frank approached them, she thought, *And I got what I wanted out of this meeting at the Peacock, right?*

Walking toward the bar, the thumping music grew louder and a wall of cologne seared her nostrils. *God, I hate this place.*

Duke was crushed. *How can they think that about me?* He stood over his kitchen sink and cracked a beer. After one sip he dumped it down the drain. He desperately wanted to forget the last few days, but he also wanted to avoid a hangover. He felt bad enough.

Both his pops and Angel believed it was possible Duke had shot his friend.

Angel. The young nursing student had been so beautiful, so perfect in a simple black dress, as clear-eyed and in-the-moment as always. He admired her. But she obviously could not say the same about him.

After the anticlimactic dinner with Angel, he'd come home and wandered around his empty house for a time, using the last of his willpower to keep from leaving scathing voice messages for Regina. *Just wait. Figure out what her game is first.*

His father banged in through the kitchen door. "I got

it." Willis held up a thumb drive. "You sure you want to see this?"

"Show me." Duke pushed his laptop across the table. He watched closely as his pops loaded the video and hit Play.

Instantly, Duke was triggered. His brain felt stuttery and his hands shook. The screaming, the loud bangs and exploding glass, the chaos of running bodies . . . The video was shot from ground level, by someone lying on the floor, with half the screen obstructed by a tabletop.

"How could Regina think to record this, Pops?"

"That woman has no heart."

The recording was shaky for the first few seconds but then steadied, with the focus on the ground a few feet away. Duke could hear Regina breathing heavily, shuddering and gasping. He felt briefly sorry for her, remembering too well the terror blanketing that room, the smell of gunpowder and hot blood in the air. The filming blurred slightly, but he could make out movement under a neighboring table, a hand reaching down and sliding a gun out of an ankle holster. The focus cleared just as he heard two more loud pops, and then—

Oh my God. No.

Duke moved quickly, grabbing a wastebasket. He retched.

A body had fallen in between the tables. Mark. The side of his face was visible, covered in blood. The Bronx Bolt catcher fluttered his eyelashes, and then, nothing.

And just past his dead friend, clearly in focus under the table, were the shoes of the killer. Gold Nike high-tops. Custom made. Stitched on the side with black and white thread, in the Bronx Bolt team's font: "The Duke."

His shoes.

Chapter Twenty

Angel did not sleep. She tossed and turned and groaned into her pillow, awake when her alarm went off Friday morning. Her mind had been fuzzy for days, trying to picture how she could handle Dr. Collins, control her resentment, get what she needed from him, and still walk away with her dignity intact.

As she cooked Jose breakfast, the smell of frying eggs made her sick. Concentrating on her son was the only thing keeping her sane.

"You have your glove, mi chiquito?"

"I'm not a baby, Mama. I have everything in my bag."

"I know, I know, you're my big man." She tousled his hair and sat down next to him at the tiny table. He was the only thing keeping her emotions in check, keeping her from becoming an ogre. "I just want to make sure you're ready for tonight. You have an intermural game, right? Dress warm. I'll bring more Claritin, or Gabriela will."

He stopped eating. "Won't you be there?"

"I'm gonna try. If I get done at the clinic early enough, I should be able to make it."

His dark brown eyes welled with tears. "I really want you to be there."

She pulled him into her lap and gave him a long cuddle. "Not as much as I want to be there. I'll make it, I promise." *Oh Lord, why did I say that?*

She got Jose off to school and then took a quick shower, crying into the hot stream hitting her face. After drying off, she picked up her deodorant, considered it for a second, and then dropped it into a drawer, next to her perfume. *I refuse to smell good for that bastard. I shouldn't have showered.*

In the mirror, her golden skin was dappled in shadow, her supple young body bent like an aged crone. Angel stood up and blazed at herself. "You will be strong. You are doing this for your son. Prostitutes do it. You will be strong, damn it." She poked her image in the chest. "Just get in there. Talk him out of it or fuck him. Do what it takes."

A knock on the front door distracted her from seesawing anger and despair.

In her terry bathrobe and a towel around her head, she strode across the living room. Not paying attention, she stepped on a scattering of Legos. "*Puñeta!*" she raged, kicking at the tiny blue and yellow and red blocks, cursing more than just her physical pain.

She opened the door.

"Were you yelling at me?" asked Duke, his eyebrows knit in concern.

She clutched the front of her robe, embarrassed, though more ashamed of the ratty old robe than of her bare flesh. He'd already seen that. She asked, "What do you want? This is a bad time."

"I'm here for your nursing skills. After this, I'll stay away, I promise."

"Nursing skills? You can't wrap your own ankle by now?"

"Can I come in?" The handsome man scanned the hallway nervously. "I'll tell you inside."

They sat awkwardly on the couch, like teenagers, space for two more people between them. She'd never noticed how lumpy the cushions were until now, or how threadbare the corduroy cover. The stains on the rug were suddenly obscene.

"So this is your place. It's nice."

"Yep, a real palace."

"Seriously, you've made it homey. I bet Jose is happy here." He gestured to the framed Botello print on the wall. "She looks like you. Very pretty. Is she related?"

"Funny guy. Jose says the same thing. It's a famous painting from Puerto Rico." She folded her arms. "Why are you here, Duke?"

He cleared his throat. "Last night, I didn't tell you . . . I need a shot." He opened the pocket of his leather coat, removing a syringe and a clear tincture bottle. "Will you do this for me?"

"Come on! After everything, now you want me to shoot you up?" She shook her head hard enough that the towel fell off and her long, damp curls sprang free. "No way!"

"This is what the doc gave me. It's unethical, and definitely would get me disbarred from the league if they knew, but it's a legal prescription." He stared at her. "I don't trust Pops to get it right. He's not a medical professional. This is important." His green eyes were earnest over his high cheekbones, his usual confidence shadowed by an air of anxiety and a deep pain. Angel hated seeing him like this.

"You admit it's 'unethical,' but you're goin' for it anyway. Duke, I told you last night, you don't need to play baseball. You're so much more than that game. And screw Regina. If she's lying, she can't hurt you."

"'If she's lying' . . . Nice. I don't have time to get into this again. Please, trust me, it's more important than ever I don't get cut. Other people are counting on me." He set the vial and syringe on the cushion. "All of this is supposed to go into my ankle, behind the outside ankle bone."

"The *lateral malleolus*," she said, proud of remembering the Latin name of the bone. She lost any positive vibes, however, when she picked up the small vial filled with clear liquid. Angel rolled the glass bottle between her fingers, frowning, wondering why her heart suddenly shivered with something that felt like grief . . . Then she knew.

She'd lost respect for Duke. As that respect receded like a wave, it also wiped out her desire to be with him. She'd been telling herself she was too busy and his life was too complicated, but that was from insecurity, while she tried to protect herself, yet, deep down, hoped they'd end up together. Now, seeing this talented man about to do something so incredibly stupid just so he could play a game and avoid conflict with Regina . . . He wasn't worth her time.

Then again, she was about to go against all her principles and throw away her self-respect. *No, the horrible thing I'm about to do, I'm doing it for Jose.* There was no one else counting on Duke, not really. Duke was doing it for Duke.

"Alright. I'm not your mama. Take off your sock and shoe." She filled the syringe, tapping the plastic to release the air bubbles, while he stripped off his shoe and put his foot on the ottoman. Pressing the tip of the needle against his flesh, she said, "Your last chance to do the right thing."

Duke's deep voice shook. "I swear to God, you the most righteous, judgmental woman . . . Just do it!"

She plunged in the needle, harder than necessary. He didn't flinch. She tossed the empty syringe and bottle into his lap and pointed at the door. She wanted him gone, before her disappointment turned to loathing. "Get out. Forget my address. I'm done doing you favors."

He rolled up his sock, narrowing his eyes at her. "You act all high and mighty, but you didn't have to go Kinley's party. You didn't have to go to the Peacock last night. Miss Martyr, that's you. Getting your picture in the paper, being seen with me, wearing expensive clothes. You liked it or you wouldn'a come back." Duke stood, towering over her. "I did you a favor. I gave your boring life a much-needed boost."

No words would form, only a garbled yell. She picked up his shoe and threw it at his head. He dodged.

"Goddamn it!" she yelled as it hit the wall, making a thwack that was not nearly as satisfying as the sound it would have made against the block he called his head.

He left without saying another word, carrying his shoe. He wasn't limping.

Angel dug a clean pair of scrubs from her drawer, dressed, and then slicked her hair back into a ponytail, still damp. No makeup, no lotion, just as she was. Cloaked in misery and hostility.

The clinic halls were slow at this time of the morning. She stalked up to Dr. Collins's office and knocked, hard. She refused to show fear.

No answer. Knocking again, with still no reply, she cracked open the door. "Dr. Collins?" She didn't hear any movement, stepped in. *Maybe he asphyxiated on his evil stench and died.*

No such luck. The office was empty.

Heavy hands dropped on her shoulders from behind. She whirled around but immediately regretted it. She was in Dr. Collins's arms. She hadn't heard him come in or shut the door.

"That's right. Shh." He pushed his skeletal length against her, holding her head to his chest as if to comfort her.

Okay. Okay. Breathe. You knew this was coming. What are you going to do?

The doctor smoothed a hand down her back, pressing her more firmly against him. His palms grazed over her buttocks before Angel gathered her wits.

She knew exactly what she was going to do: quit, no matter the loss. Nothing was worth the humiliation and disgust she felt right now, for him and for herself. She wrenched against the doctor, but his arms became locked steel. One hand cupped her bottom and squeezed.

Angel grunted and swung to the side. The sudden movement broke his hold, but he managed to capture her forearm before she was completely free, his encircling fingers a painful vise just above her wrist.

She quieted herself. "Let me go," she said calmly, glaring up into his face. *I will get control here.*

Instead, he forced her hand to the hardened lump in his pants.

Rubbing Angel's palm back and forth over his zipper, he arched into her. Sweat glistened at his temples, his lips a bright red against his pale skin. The doctor's twisted grin frightened her more than his hold on her. Revolted, she tried to yank her hand free.

"This isn't going to happen!" she whisper-yelled at him, her mind razor sharp for the first time in days. "Let the fuck go!"

"Careful, darlin'," Dr. Collins drawled in his faux southern accent, pressing himself harder against her open hand, holding her wrist so tightly her hand ached and tingled from lack of circulation. "Or I won't give you your present."

Suddenly, his fingers still biting into her wrist, he moved her hand from his crotch up to his face. Angel tried to slap at him with her other hand, but he ignored it; the angle was too awkward to do any damage. Instead, he shut his eyes, revealing veiny, fluttery eyelids and white eyelashes. Then he placed his papery lips in the center of her palm.

She jumped when he ran the tip of his tongue out, traced a wet circle on her flesh. The doctor sighed. "An appetizer. I knew you'd taste good."

She jerked frantically.

Then he opened his eyes and released her.

She was so stunned—by the freedom, but also by the weird hand licking—that her feet were frozen for a beat. After what felt like an eternity, she jumped behind a chair, giving herself a buffer, and eyed the door, dithering over her options. *If I go now, I'm not getting my evaluation. Damn sure I'm gonna kick him in his saggy balls if he tries to get close. He's not getting the drop on me again.*

Turning away, the doctor picked up an inhaler from the desk. Then he did surprise her, again, this time by throwing the inhaler at her.

Not expecting an object to come flying her way, Angel didn't lift her hands. The canister hit her chest with a thump and then dropped to the ground. She gasped. "What the hell is wrong with you?"

He smirked and moved behind his desk.

The ball of hate and self-loathing in her throat only grew harder and larger as she bent to retrieve the medicine and struggled to corral her rage. It popped and bubbled and sparked from the ends of her hair. If she'd been at the club, or anywhere else, she'd never let anyone get away with what Dr. Collins had done to her in the last few minutes. She'd bust their ass and pay for the consequences later.

She was afraid of Dr. Collins and what he could do. But did her response have to be an all-or-nothing thing, an all-out attack or total submission?

"You know what?" she said as she stood. "I've worked hard for this clinic. For you. I deserve to pass the practicum without you molesting me." Angel shuddered. She couldn't decide whether the touch of his penis or of his tongue was the most horrifying. "And you should be helping Jose out of the goodness of your heart. I don't get you. You've settled with Duke—you should be happy."

Dr. Collins ignored her, dropping into his desk chair

and picking up a pen as if everything were normal. The monster who dwelled inside his pasty skin now hid behind a professional demeanor.

"I have here two copies of your final evaluation. Both are signed and dated. One is a pass. The other is a fail." He tapped a stack of papers with the gold Cross pen. "You need this by the end the day, correct?"

"I—"

"And you mentioned Jose. You'd rather see him go without medicine than satisfy an old man?"

"You are a terrible human being."

"Come back at the end of your shift, princess. We'll see which evaluation you choose then."

She trembled with fury. Her attention narrowed to the pen in his hand. She could stab him in the eye with it. Better yet, the throat. His dark blue external jugular vein visibly throbbed as it ran over the neck's sternocleidomastoid muscle and under his tissue-thin, white-pebbled skin. She'd have to swing hard and be accurate, but she could do it.

Then anguish swamped her, draining her strength and energy. She'd thought she'd have the nightmare over by the time she left this office. Only the image of blood spurting from his jugular as he choked for air calmed her breathing. She backed toward the door.

"You're not touching me again, *pendejo.*" Her voice came out as a low creak.

"Aren't I?" He sniggered and patted the evaluations.

The student nurse let herself out, though her arms and legs were so heavy she barely had enough strength to turn the knob. But fear that he was behind her, reaching to pull her back into his lair, shot adrenaline into her system; she sprinted down the hall to the locker room. Blinded by tears, she didn't make it. Her vomit hit the wall next to the door, splattering her face and hair.

A slight wind kicked up a puff of dust on the stadium infield, cooling Duke's face as he loped onto the diamond.

When the pitcher realized he had zero pain, for the first time in months, he stretched his legs and ran, sprinting across the dirt. Pure joy blasted through his body. He made it to second base before it struck him that he might be wasting a short-lived reprieve. He slowed up, sauntered to the pitcher's mound, exuding confidence and grace. The field and stands were empty, but he knew he wasn't alone. He was putting on a show, but it felt right, being able to move and act like the man he used to be. *And I will be that man again*, he told himself. Life seemed so much brighter.

And then the glass elevator descended from the top of the stadium. The owner's suite.

The Bronx Bolts' general manager, the general manager, and the owner stepped off the platform, accompanied by the batting coach and the head team doctor. No one was smiling. The manager approached the mound while Duke and the batter warmed up.

"Hey, Skip."

"Duke." The manager spit to the side. "You ready?"

The pitcher grinned. He felt good. Strong. "You'll see. I'm betta than ever. I won't let you down."

The man tugged on his cap. "We'll see."

Duke watched him jog back to the small group waiting in the dugout. The batter took another practice swing and then stepped up to the plate, giving Duke the nod. Duke breathed in and out, deeply, then went into his stance, one leg up, his elbow going back—

There was a buzz at the back of his brain that suddenly became very loud. He realized he'd been hearing it for a while now but he'd been ignoring it. *What is that?* He tilted his head, patted his ear. Still there. He dropped his stance and smacked at his head. The batter gaped at him like he was crazy. Duke shrugged and offered the guy a grin, but the buzz persisted.

What in the hell? He pounded his fist into his baseball glove, willing the high-pitched sound to go away. *Like I need this right now. About to give the biggest performance of my life.* And then he knew what it was.

His sense of right was making itself known. His conscience had woken up.

His whole life, he'd fought hard to be acknowledged. When he found it was pitching that earned him recognition, adoration, he'd worked even harder. He lived and breathed baseball, until the game and his role in it became a major part of his psyche. When he was on the mound, he wasn't faking it. It wasn't a *performance*. It was him, the raw talent he'd built into a skill, the man he'd worked to become.

Angel's right. I can't cheat now. I'd never be able to look at myself in the mirror again.

Stepping off the mound, Duke slowly pulled the glove from his hand, dropped it on the pitcher's plate. He caressed the leather of the ball one more time, the red stitches catching at the calluses on his fingertips. Then he let the ball fall into the glove.

He and the manager exchanged a long look. Sadness washed over the manager's face when he realized what was happening; the older man offered a single nod and turned away. Duke, unable to bear the shame, broke into a jog, heading for the locker room.

From behind him, the famous pitcher heard loud conversation boiling out of the dugout, and then the Bronx Bolts' owner shouting after him. The harsh words bounced around the empty Bronx Bolt Stadium.

Duke left the field with the echoes pinging around inside his skull.

You're fired, you're fired, you're fired . . .

Chapter Twenty-one

Angel sat on the floor of a shower stall in the clinic's female locker room; it was her second time crying in the shower that day.

She couldn't stop. She'd been pushed around before. She'd touched a dick before. And this time she'd stuck up for herself and broke free before the man could do any real damage. But that she had to . . . that she had to fight to maintain her dignity and space. That the fight was against someone who was supposed to be not only her boss but also her mentor in a career devoted to helping others. That she had to fight against a fellow human being, one who had taken away her power to choose, or even move. Worst of all was that she had to fight but then she'd been forced to pull her punches, to struggle, but not enough to anger him, just in case he decided to hurt her career. Or hurt her physically.

Her altercation with the doctor had been short, but it was a violation. An exhausting reminder that women fight or they suffer. And sometimes they fight *and* suffer.

I'm not letting this happen. I'm not having sex for his signature. I will find a way to provide for Jose, but I'm not giving up my soul to do it.

She inched herself up the shower wall. *I'm not letting it happen. No rape.* She wasn't going to get her nurse's license. She would deal with it, standing up, straight and proud. *But I'm also going to deal with Dr. Collins.* How many women had he defiled over the years? Dozens? More? She didn't have a plan, but she'd have some free time to come up with something, what with school over next week and no more clinic hours. *Maybe I'll start studying the law between bartending shifts . . .*

Rage, her familiar friend, gave her a hand up, pushing desolation back into a corner. She rinsed the salt off her face, made sure the vomit was gone from her hair, and stepped out of the shower.

Toweling off, she realized she'd also have more time for Jose.

Starting now.

She dropped her pass on the charge nurse's desk and trotted to the back doors. As she threw them open, a wind whistled past her. And then the alarm went off. It felt fitting, to disappear down the alley with an undulating horn to send her on her way. It harmonized with the screaming in her head.

·   ·   ·

Duke shed his practice jersey in the parking lot, striding across acres of gray pavement interrupted only by white lines to mark the empty spaces, and the occasional pothole or dirty Styrofoam cup. In a moment of giddiness, free of games and lies, he dropped the shirt on the hood of a maintenance man's pickup, a well-used Datsun with ladders and dead tree limbs in the back. *Get it on eBay quick, buddy, while it's still worth something.*

"Roland," he said into his phone, walking toward the 161st Street subway station, "I don't know where you are, but meet me at my house in an hour. We've got to talk."

He hung up, peering around him as he made his way onto the concourse, merging with the streams of city dwellers making their way in and out of the Bronx. No one paid him any attention; he was simply another guy in the crowd. The body odor and cigarette smoke, the crying of babies and the shrieking of brakes on the rails, the gooey remnants of gum on the handrails, teenagers and office workers and waitresses pushing past him . . .

Horror flooded through him as he boarded the train, carried by the crush of people. He grunted with the pain of it. This was who he was now. He was a nobody on the street, and he had no woman, no family, waiting for him at home. Right back where he'd started out. Except, as a kid, he'd ride the subways to practices and games with the goal of a better life on the horizon. What was he working toward now? Manager at McDonald's?

As the train sped up away from the stadium, he felt

hopeless. He had to get his money back from Regina somehow. Otherwise, he was broke *and* without a career. Behind his reflection, warehouses and apartment buildings rushed by. They were leaving the past, hurtling into a blurred future.

Gabriela glanced up over the head of a haircutting client and frowned at Angel, disheveled, coming in the salon door. "What have we got goin' on here?"

Angel let out a sob and stumbled toward the Dominican hairdresser.

Gabriela threw down her scissors, narrowly missing the startled woman in the chair, and rushed to gather up Angel. "Oh my God! Oh my God! What is it?"

The young woman could only cry, shuddering great heaving breaths, as Gabriela rocked her.

"Just tell me, Jose is okay?"

Angel nodded against her shoulder. She leaned in, putting her weight on her friend, and cried harder. "Ye-e-s-s, he's fine," she finally hitched out, "but I failed my pra-a-ctic-c-um." More sobs. Gabriela simply took it in without saying a word, holding her close. Everything Angel had held on to for the past week—maybe the last few years— could not be contained any longer. Now that she'd finally given in and sought support from her friend, she found she couldn't help but let the dam continue to crumble. There was no stopping the flood of emotions and tears, but Gabriela stayed with her, steadying her, cooing, stroking her hair. The unconditional love from her friend just made Angel cry even more.

"Why we meeting here, bro?" Roland asked. "Thought you wanted to get some lunch."

The two professional athletes sat a wide stone table on the back patio at Duke's house, next to a heated pool. Steam rose off the smooth sheen, fading into the watery sunlight.

Duke cracked open two beers and offered him one. "We need to talk, without a scene."

"What the hell you playin' at?"

Taking out his phone, Duke laid it in front of Roland. He pressed Play on the video file he'd loaded earlier. Faint screams and gunfire could be heard coming from the tinny speaker.

Roland turned gray. He jammed his fingers wildly at the screen, trying to turn it off. "No!"

Duke slid it out of his reach.

"Where'd you get this?"

"Wait . . . Okay. Here." Duke paused the recording. There was Mark on the floor. Dead. "Do you see what I see, Roland?"

"You're sick, man," Roland growled. "Why you doin' this?"

Duke was grim. "Look behind Mark. Under the table. See the shoes?"

Roland nodded, but his eyes were shut.

"Those are my shoes. My gold high-tops." Duke hit Rewind, held up the screen. "Open your eyes."

Then he tapped Play again. They both watched as the person in the gold shoes, the top half of his body hidden by a table, reached to his ankle for a gun and brought up the weapon. Two shots were heard. Mark fell to the ground. Duke hit Stop. "Those are my high-tops. But you're the shooter, Roland. You were wearing my shoes that night."

"How did you—"

"You're asking how I got this? That's what you're worried about? Not that you committed murder? You killed our friend!"

The big man's face pinched in agony. "No, it wasn't like that. It was an accident!" He was hyperventilating. "I'd do anything to go back in time. You gotta believe me, I had nothin' but love for that guy. I'd never shoot Mark."

"But you did. And then you ran away."

"You have no idea!" Roland covered his face with his hands. "I been living in hell, trying to figure out what went wrong."

"Living. You've been living." Duke put the phone in his pocket. "Mark has not. And, so's you know, Regina is the one who recorded this. Only she thinks what she was watching was *me* shooting Mark. She's been blackmailing my pops, threatening to give this to the cops."

"No!" Roland lifted his head and blinked at him, tears on his cheeks. "No, that can't be right."

"Oh, but it is. She wiped out my savings before Pops got around to telling me about it. Now you're gonna help me get that money back."

Roland groaned, smacked his head. "Duke. She's been blackmailing *me* since that night. She knows it was me."

"What . . . I don't understand . . ." Duke's head exploded; it felt like a bolt of lightning struck him in the temple. He saw everything in that painful flash. *I should have realized.* She'd known Roland had borrowed Duke's shoes that night, after the game in Chicago. They'd all laughed—Duke, Roland, Mark, and Regina—during the cab ride to the club, when Roland got into the front with the driver and the man thought the famous hitter was the Duke, thanks to the stitching on the side of the shoes.

"You didn't know she was trickin' Pops?" Duke asked.

"No! I figured she knew I did it, so it was just between us."

Duke turned off the phone and slid it into his jacket pocket. "Crazy. That is some crazy shit. That woman is cold." He kicked back from the table. "Why didn't you just tell the cops that night? If it was an accident?"

"I'm a black man with a gun. No permit. No way they believing me. At the very least I'd have been on trial forever. Brother, I was trying to protect us! I was shooting at one of those maniacs when Mark jumped into my line of fire." He mashed the heel of his hand into his eye. "I can't forget it. It's in my head, day and night." His voice fell into whining. "But it was an accident. I wasn't about to go to prison for something I didn't start."

"So you ditched me and Regina? Ran away and left us, even when I'd been shot? And then when the cops were lookin' at me, you just kept quiet?"

"What was I supposed to do? No one was going to believe me! I knew you'd be fine, you always are."

"Oh, am I? Am I fine?"

"Well, you still playing, ain't you? I helped you get drugs for your ankle . . ."

"I didn't go through with it. It wasn't right." Duke stared at a bank of clouds. "I'm off the team. And I'm broke, thanks to you and Regina."

"Me? She's the one blackmailing you!"

"If you'd come forward, instead of being a coward, she wouldn't have been able to blackmail either of us. Does Kinley know what's going on?"

"Not really. She says I been messed up by Mark's death. Which is true, but not in the way she thinks. I was agitated, playin' recklessly, until I got hurt." Roland put a hand to his wrist. "I deserved what I got. I deserved to lose my spot at the show." He started crying again.

Duke had a hard time arguing the point. "What about money? How much you pay her?"

"I don't even know. Millions. Kinley knows there's

money missing, but she don't know how much or why. She did accuse me of spending it on Regina, but as a mistress, not a fuckin' grifter."

"That's right! Why in the hell *were* you bangin' that evil thing? What were you thinkin'?"

"She made me."

Duke looked at him sharply. "Roland, you the biggest pussy I know."

"What are you going to do?"

"No, Roland, what are *you* going to do?" Duke leaned in. "You don't confess, Regina keeps on taking money from you. Me, there's nothing left . . . But she doesn't know that we've found out her double deal. She doesn't know I've seen the video, that I know how she put one over on Pops. She is going to panic when she finds out—you know that, right? She'll turn it over to the cops. They'll think it was me, Roland. Me. My shoes. She'll *say* it was me. Then she can keep bribing you while I'm in fuckin' jail. So. What are you going to do?"

Roland stood up abruptly. "I gotta think." His eyes were rolling like a wild horse.

Duke jumped up. "Easy there. Keep your head."

Roland took off at a run, leaping over the side gate on the back fence as Duke watched in astonishment. Only seconds passed before he heard a car door slam and a car peel out from in front of his house.

Willis came out of the house. "That was some messed-up shit."

"Did you get it?"

"Yeah. I got him." His father held up a small recorder. "But you really going to turn him in? He'll go away for a long time, everything he's done."

"Pops, I'm gonna let him turn himself in. That's what I'm hopin', anyway. But if Regina tries to turn on me before then, I gotta be ready. I'm not goin' down for something I didn't do."

"Can you believe the balls on that woman? How she ever thought she was going to keep a double scam going is beyond me. I can't believe I fell for it in the first place. I should have known that wasn't you on the video. You aren't a killer, Duke. I know that. You're a decent boy."

Duke waited quietly, knowing there was a dig coming. Willis wasn't going to let this end without explaining to Duke how this was his fault.

"I let fear of losing money get in the way of common sense. Of family. I'm ashamed of myself. I'm gonna make this right."

Duke was shocked. "We'll do it together, Pops."

"I guess you have the time now, huh?" Willis put a hand on his shoulder. "I'm sorry about the Bronx Bolts. You did the right thing. I'm not as brave; I would have done anything to keep that job. But I know you—you'd have been unhappy, using drugs to make yourself look good. You don't need that bullshit. You *are* good. You'll heal, come back better than ever."

Never in Duke's years had Willis complimented him.

Even when the Bronx Bolt pitcher was at the height of his career, he'd never been good enough. Instead, Willis had constantly told him how much of a letdown he was, even while Duke was setting up his pops with a luxurious suite and a job. Duke rubbed a hand across his face, extremely tired, but a small bit of his heart was healed.

"Pops, that ship has sailed. Skip's done with me. I'll figure it out. Maybe they'll take me on a farm team somewhere."

Willis and Duke walked inside together, into their home, even if it was only for a little while longer. "But I don't want to think about what I've lost anymore, not right now."

Duke was getting ready to drop onto the couch when he changed his mind.

"Before I jump into any other mess, I need some closure. I got to apologize to Angel, thank her for bein' real. I think I really hurt her." Remorse swept through him. Shame and guilt. For letting himself wallow in self-pity, for not taking care of his wounds, for making immature and harmful choices. For wasting his God-given talents. And for using Angel. "She was the only one helping me out of kindness, and tellin' me what I needed to hear."

He left Willis at the house and drove to the clinic. Duke was excited to tell Angel what he'd done. That she didn't have to be disappointed in him. At the front desk, though, Theresa told him the beautiful woman was gone. He was too late.

The pink-faced nursing student beckoned him close. "She just took off, leaving us shorthanded. Dr. Collins is on the rampage, yellin' at all of us."

"Why'd she leave?"

"I don't know!" Theresa shook her head, concerned. "She didn't say anything to me. The doctor's asked me, like, six times if she's talked to me, but no." She glanced around and leaned in even closer. "He seems obsessed. You know what I'm sayin', homey?"

Duke snorted. "You think you gangsta?" He laughed, but the poor girl blushed so hard he figured he could roast a marshmallow on her face. "You fine, girl. I'm just givin' you a bad time. Anyway, should I be worried about Angel?"

"I'd be more worried about Collins. I think he's feeling rejected."

"Why—"

"Theresa! Those urine samples aren't going to test themselves. Get going," said the charge nurse, scowling at Duke with a classic old-lady glare. Theresa gave him a sorrowful shrug and scurried off.

"Wait—" he said. *Why would Mr. Freaky Freak feel rejected?* As Duke walked out, he thought about how the doc acted around Angel, always touching her. *There's no way she's interested in that old guy. Right?*

He decided to drive down Jerome Avenue, see if he could catch Angel at her apartment. When he got to the salon, however, it was closed. There was a note: *Gone to the baseball game!*

.   .   .

It was cold. Damn cold. Ass-cheek-frozen cold.

Angel was sure she was losing weight watching these preseason games, due to nonstop shivering even with a coat. *I should have changed out of my scrubs.* There was sun shining on the field at the elementary school, but the wintery breeze blowing through the Bronx streets turned the metal benches into ice makers.

"Mama!" Jose waved as he ran past her with his team. When he'd spotted her, his face had lit up. It warmed her heart to see him so happy simply because she was there. *I did one thing right today.*

"You go, baby!" Gabriela yelled, shouting excitedly into Angel's ear. She'd closed down her business to be with Angel on the sidelines of Jose's game, even though it was just an intermural game so Angel wasn't about to say a word about her exuberance. She didn't have the energy to do much but breathe, anyway.

Angel tried to rally, to put everything but Jose out of her mind. But it was so hard. As Jose's team took their turn at bat, she could barely focus. When they switched to the field before Jose could bat, she was relieved, not sure she had the energy to worry about him getting struck out.

Her brain continued to be sluggish. Toward the end of the second inning, her mind played tricks, making her think she saw Duke strolling along the baseline fence, cheering on the kids. The vision seemed so real when the imaginary ballplayer then purposefully strode toward their small set of stands behind Jose's dugout.

"Angel?"

She stared at the apparition as it excused its way through benches tight with incredulous, gaping parents. It even sounded like Duke. When it got up close and waved a hand in front of her face and said, "Can't you hear me?" she jumped.

"Duke?" she whispered. *Is that Duke? I'm not crazy?* Louder, she said, "What are you doing here?"

"What she means," said Gabriela, leaning across Angel's lap, "is what in the hell are *you* doing here?" Then she batted her eyelashes coyly and said, "But you know I love ya, right?" However, after Angel stared fixedly at her friend, the hairdresser added, "Ah, I mean, I don't love you. You're an asshole."

Duke sat down beside Angel. "Yes, Gabriela, I know. I'm sorry. Do you hear that, Angel? I'm sorry?"

All around them was a whispering rustle as the other adults tried to decide whether the new man in their midst, who looked an awful lot like a famous Bronx Bolt, was really the Duke.

Why is he bothering to apologize to me? I don't understand why he doesn't just leave me alone. She struggled with a response, but Gabriela, who still leaned across her, said, "She's not talkin' to you. You just take your conceited ass right on outta here. We don't need you."

"I know, I know. I said and did terrible things. But I

wanted you to know, Angel, I didn't go through with it.
You were right; it wasn't worth it. I'm not playing anymore."

There was a collective gasp from the group around
them. Duke ignored his audience.

Angel turned her head slowly, dragging her gaze across
the upturned, curious faces to meet his gaze. She was sure
she had misheard him, since his features were peaceful.
Finally allowing herself to stare into those green eyes,
which were serene, intent on her, she felt tears welling. *I
can't seem to stop crying today.*

"Really?"

Duke nodded. "I don't want to be a fake. I want to win
because of the talent God gave me and the skills I've worked
hard to perfect. I want people to like me because of who
I am, for real."

"Duke! No! Don't quit!" said one unnerved dad, twisting around in his seat.

His wife shushed the man, embarrassed. Gabriela said,
"What is wrong with you people? Mind your own damn
business. You all a bunch of rubes, I swear."

While the hairdresser continued to berate those closest to them, Duke mouthed "Sorry" to the crowd, but then
he slid closer to Angel, put his head next to hers, and spoke
quietly, earnestly, his breath soft on her cheek. She wanted
to caress the spot.

"I need to keep it real for myself. I know that now. I'm
woke. I want to live like Mark did, and you, proud of my

choices. Maybe even someday be a role model for kids like Jose." He shrugged, worry creasing his mouth. His voice dropped so low, she had to lean in to him to hear. "I'm not sure what I'm going to do, but I have to get my house in order before I can deal with that."

"You gave up so much." She put a hand on his knee, empathy blasting through her. *I totally understand how it feels to abandon something you've worked so hard for.* "It doesn't really matter what I think, but you did the right thing. I'll be proud if Jose grows up to make that kind of choice."

"It does matter what you think! I'm sorry I've made you think otherwise." He put his hand on top of hers. "You've already modeled love and sacrifice for your little man. I've never had to care for anyone but myself. Look what you've done for him."

She pulled away then, coming back to her senses. She was unsure and unhappy, and that was in part because of him taking advantage of her friendship, which she hadn't offered to anyone in a very long time. She was glad he'd been honest with his boss, but she had her own problems. She didn't know him and he didn't know her, not really. He couldn't. He didn't have the capability to care about others, and she didn't have the strength to show him how. She clasped her hands together, pinching the web of skin, trying to keep the composure she'd fought hard to regain before leaving Gabriela's salon.

He put a finger under her chin, made her look at him. "What's going on, Angel? I understand you being mad at me, but why didn't you do your practicum thing?" When her glistening eyes widened in surprise, he said, "Your friend at the clinic told me you missed some review. Is it that son of a bitch Collins? She said he was mad at you." He licked his lips. "You didn't have something going with that guy, did you?"

"Sweet Jesus, boy, how could you ask that?" hissed Gabriela, unable to stop herself from jumping in. "You have no damn idea what is going on."

"Gabriela, it's alright." Angel regretted telling her what had happened. She needed to deal with this in her own way. She reached up to push Gabriela into her seat, but quickly put her hand back in her lap and tugged her sleeve into place. Angel didn't want to have to answer questions about the dark bruises circling her wrist.

"No, it's not. I'm goin' to beat that man's ass into the ground, then—"

"Stop, Gabriela."

"No, don't stop, Gabriela. Tell me what you're talking about." Duke's eyes were narrowed. "Angel, seriously, what is happening?"

There was a commotion on the field. The batter was warming up, but the pitcher for Jose's team was paying attention to something behind him. A teammate. The boy playing shortstop had dropped to the ground without warning. The pitcher yelled at him, but the boy stayed on the ground, not moving.

"Is that—"

Angel leapt to her feet. "Jose!" she screamed.

She clawed at her pocket and, finding his inhaler, almost fell down the bleachers as she clambered over spectators to get to the ground. A chain-link fence stopped her rush forward. She frantically searched for a way in, but someone grabbed the inhaler from her hand. Next to her, Duke grabbed the top of the chest-high fence and vaulted over, his feet already moving when he landed.

Duke streaked across the diamond to the boy, reaching him before the coaches did.

Gabriela, behind her, shouted at a 911 operator on the phone.

Angel was stuck, unable to help, unable to get to her baby, until something broke inside of her. A fog cleared. She ran to the side entrance of the closest dugout, pushed through the milling group of anxious boys, and popped onto the field. There were sirens wailing in the distance.

By the time she reached the cluster of people around Jose, she could see he was struggling, turning blue around his lips. He was conscious, but his breath came in short, hard gasps, no air coming out, his hands scrabbling at his throat. Duke, kneeling beside him, a hand under his head, held up the inhaler. "I gave it to him. It's not doing anything."

The ambulance screeched up to the edge of the field. They were more than a football field of distance away, stopped behind a gate not wide enough to drive through.

She saw Duke notice the EMTs in the distance, look at Jose, and then look at her.

"Yes! Go!" she shouted.

Duke gathered the seven-year-old in his arms and took off at a dead sprint, his long legs flying.

"Oh God! Oh God! Oh God!" she cried out, sparks of terror coming from her as she raced after them. She had no idea if she was cursing or praying, maybe both, watching Duke and her dying boy pull farther and farther away.

Chapter Twenty-two

"You're not allowed—"

Angel shoved the much-larger EMT aside. "You'll have to arrest me."

She jumped up into the ambulance, beside another EMT, who was securing Jose's stretcher to the wall. To him she said, "I'm a nurse. I won't get in your way."

The young bearded man reset the oxygen mask over Jose's small face and then cast his attention to the woman behind the wheel. The driver was obviously the boss, despite her spiky blue hair and tattooed neck.

Angel put a hand on Jose's thigh, squeezing, wishing he'd open his eyes. His face was white, his lips blue. "I'm here, baby." To the driver, she said with icy steel, "I'm not getting off. Let's go."

The driver sighed and nodded back to the EMT, saying, "Okay, lady, but you strap yourself in."

The alert on Jose bleated. He was crashing.

Duke sat on the curb alongside the elementary school, unsure of what to do. Gabriela came jogging up to him. Breathing hard, she said, "Come on. Let's go. Did you drive? Do you know what hospital they're going to?"

He pointed to his car, across the street. "That's mine. They went to University."

"Give me your keys."

He handed them over mutely. "I'm gonna need you to help me walk."

As she wove them dangerously through traffic, honking and yelling at drivers, his wrecked ankle burned. It was in the background, though, against the fervent prayers he was saying for Jose. He couldn't forget how the boy's small body had felt, flopping against him as he ran as fast as he could toward the ambulance. He'd felt Jose shudder and buck, trying to breathe. Duke would have ripped out his lungs that very second, would have given his own life, if it would have helped Jose.

When they drove into the hospital's emergency bay, Gabriela let out a small scream.

They saw the parked ambulance, the back doors flung open. Jose's gurney was being rushed through the doors—with Angel straddling his small body, counting, as she repetitively compressed his chest. She was performing CPR.

Angel's arms and chest ached after ten minutes of compressions. She didn't know how emergency responders did it, keeping up the hard, measured pushing as often as they did on those long ambulance rides.

When Jose had quit breathing, and then his heart stopped, Angel scrambled on top of him without a second thought. She was grateful the EMT didn't stop her; instead, he took off Jose's oxygen mask and replaced it with a bag, pumping out the breaths on her count. The driver had driven like the tires were on fire, but Angel simply hooked her feet into the swaying cot's rails and used her ankles and thighs to stay in place, wishing only that the ambulance could go faster.

Now, standing aside as the doctors worked over him in the emergency room, she felt her heart calm. Her brain slowed. She found peace. She knew what she was going to do.

She was going to kill herself. If they couldn't bring him back around. The instant they pronounced him, she was going to slip into a maintenance closet, find a bottle of Drano, and make sure she followed him into the light. If her baby had to go, so would she.

"Got him!" a bald-headed doctor crowed.

She heard Jose, on the gurney, take in a large breath,

then cough, then gag. It was the most beautiful sound she'd ever heard, the singing of angels.

Angel sat outside the pediatric ICU with Gabriela on one side, Duke on the other. Everything was surreal. An intern had stopped to ask the Bronx Bolt for an autograph, but Gabriela barked at the man like a rabid dog and he skittered away.

"Don't bother, Gabriela," Duke said over Angel's head. "Some people just don't get it. They'll interrupt the most personal moments. They don't care."

"I guess you won't miss that."

They were all quiet again.

Then a doctor came out, her wrinkled face tired. "Ms. Gomez?" she said to the group.

Angel jumped up. "How is he? Is he okay?"

"He is alive; he is back to breathing on his own. But . . . he's not waking up."

Gabriela grabbed the doctor's arm. "My Lord, he's in a coma?"

The doctor patted her hand, then gently removed it. "It's far too early to say he's in a coma. I'm the head of pediatrics here, and I believe his brain may just need rest, so let's give him some time. I know it's scary, and I'm not going to sugarcoat it. There is reason to be concerned."

Angel's legs felt weak. Duke slid an arm around her; it was the only reason she didn't fall.

"On the other hand," the doctor continued, "he was

never completely without oxygen, thanks to your CPR. You got him to us very quickly, and we have him stable. For now, we're just going to sit tight, watch him closely. We'll reassess in an hour or two, decide if we need to change our plan." The doctor tucked a clipboard under her arm. "Ms. Gomez, I know it's hard. But we're going to do our very best to help your boy."

"Oh." It was all she could say. There was so much more. The only other thing she could push out, though, was a strangled, "Thank you."

"You think this was triggered by his asthma, correct? Has he been using his inhaler?"

"Yes. Jose had one on him. He used it right before his game. Duke gave him another dose when he first collapsed."

Next to her, she felt Duke recoil. He dug the inhaler out of his pocket and handed it to the doctor. "I hope to God it wasn't my fault. I put it into his mouth and pushed down at least three times." He rubbed his chin. "I don't know, was that too much? Did I do it wrong?"

The doctor frowned. "No, no, it sounds like you did what you could." She appraised the inhaler. Flipping it over, scrutinizing the label, her frown grew deeper. "Where'd you get this? It's not marked by a pharmacy or medical office."

"Our doctor gave it to us. Dr. Collins, in Mount Eden, at the clinic."

"Huh." She put it in her pocket. "You can go in to see

Jose now, in room 2C. I think it's good you talk to him. But stay positive."

As the three of them walked into the pediatric ICU, through the locked double doors and past the desk, the doctor touched Angel's arm lightly, speaking quietly. "Can I talk to you for a sec?"

Duke followed Gabriela into Jose's room, surprised that no one stopped him to ask if he was family. The machinery and computers provided a light hum and a low, constant beep. *I suppose that's his heart. Please keep beating.*

Gabriela, her face white, caught his eye. He put an arm around her and walked with her to Jose's side. "We're here, little buddy. It's me, Duke." He nudged Gabriela.

The hairdresser started crying. Duke said quietly, in her ear, "We've got to be strong. Okay? For both of them." Gabriela nodded, dried her tears, and gently took Jose's hand. Duke knew she loved Jose like her own family and that she kept her mouth closed because she'd be unable to control her tears if she didn't. Duke totally understood— he felt the same.

Angel swept in and moved directly to her son. Settling in next to him, gingerly working her arm around his head and the tubes, she said, "I'm right here, mi *chiquito*. Right here. I was talking to the doctor. She says you are going to be just fine and it's okay if you take this little rest."

Duke was proud of her. The young mother's voice hitched at the end, but she maintained control. Angel was going to be what Jose needed. He watched as she smoothed the hair and perspiration off her son's forehead, laid her cheek against his pale skin. Softly, she repeated, "She says you're going to be okay."

But Duke had also seen the dark rage in her eyes as she entered the room. He hoped it didn't mean there really was something wrong with Jose. Or that *he* had anything to do with it. He'd never forgive himself.

Chapter Twenty-three

The rhythmic noises of the hospital equipment and the soothing murmurs of the women as they caressed Jose were hypnotic, but terror and the pain in Duke's ankle kept him awake. His phone rang, startling him. "I'm sorry, guys. Didn't realize I had it on."

They weren't paying any attention to him.

It was Kinley on the phone. No one noticed when Duke limped out into the hall and leaned against the wall of the ICU; it was unbearable to put any weight on his ankle. But right now seemed like the wrong time to complain. He'd make sure the kid was okay, then he'd see somebody. Not Dr. Collins. A real doctor. No need to hide anymore.

"Duke!" Kinley said, before he could even say hello. "I saw you on the news! Is that little boy okay?"

He groaned. "Are you kidding me?"

"You saved a kid's life, that's what the newscasters are

saying. There's footage of you running with him, taking him to an ambulance. He looked like he was unconscious."

"It's Jose, Angel's son. I'm at the hospital with him and his mom right now." Duke put a hand over his eyes, dropped his voice. "He's not waking up, Kinley. It's pretty awful."

"I'm coming over. I'm already on my way."

"No—"

She'd hung up.

Out in the waiting area, he barely made it to the chairs without falling. It felt like he'd been shot minutes ago, not months ago.

After dropping into the seat, he glanced up to find Kinley coming down the hall in a red wool suit. He grumbled, "You said you were on your way, not here already."

"Duke! You can't walk? Oh no!" Kinley sat next to him. She knew exactly what it meant for an athlete to be hurt during the season.

"Yeah. I re-tore everything." He gripped the arms of the chair and blew out his breath. At least he could finally admit it in the open. "Good thing I quit this morning or I'd be fired. Well, they might have fired me, but I quit first."

Kinley leaned forward, perplexed. "What are you talking about? What's going on?"

"It's a long story. Suffice it to say, my ankle was not healing right. I wasn't going to be able to play anyway. This," he pointed to the purple and swollen tissue, "is just the final nail in the coffin. But, like I said, I was already dead. It doesn't matter."

"And Jose? Poor Angel! Please tell me he's okay."

"It's pretty scary. How'd you know we were here, anyway?"

"News crews are reporting from the main lobby."

"Of course they are. Jose had an asthma attack during his baseball game and stopped breathing on the way here. He's still unconscious. We're waiting to see if he's going to recover."

"Jesus. What a day." She paused. "You need to know, though, there's more. Roland told me everything." When Duke raised his eyebrows, she nodded. "About Regina, about the money, and about Mark."

He felt the air in his chest ball up. "He told you he killed Mark?"

"Yes, he showed me the video, admitted he ran away like a little bitch." She wiped her hands together, as if wiping off dirt. "I took a copy of the video and then I made him call the police, Duke. I was in the room with him, on the speakerphone. Our lawyers conferenced in. Roland admitted to it all. And I made sure the detective was clear on the blackmailing angle."

"I can't believe it." Duke took a moment to process and then said, "Make sure you talk to Pops. He has Roland on tape, admitting he did it, and that he knew I was innocent And Pops also has threatening letters from that nutbag Regina. The extortionist even signed her name."

Kinley snorted. "Of course she did. No one has ever accused Roland of being a genius, but Regina may just be a rung below him."

"I think Roland was a coward, and I can't forgive him for killing Mark," Duke said darkly, "but what Regina's been doing . . . it's crazy. She's sick. How did we not see it?"

"I know. She wasn't always nice, but I had no idea she was straight-up evil." Kinley brought her phone out, set it in her lap. "Regina probably can't pay back what she's stolen, but it's her life behind bars that I want, anyway. I want to know that her beautiful body is going to wither, that she'll get fat and her tits will sag, sitting on an uncomfortable bunk reading old *Redbook* magazines, and that the prisoners treat the stuck-up bitch like they do the pedophiles and baby killers."

"But what about Roland?" said Duke. "He's gonna go to prison, too."

"And don't you think he should? He might have shot Mark on accident, but when he ran away, he started a chain of events and he did nothing to stop it, even when it hurt you."

"Remind me not to piss you off, Kinley. That's your husband you're talking about."

"It was time to upgrade, anyway." She held up her phone. "So, who gets to tell Regina the police are on their way. You? Or me?"

•   •   •

Angel kissed Jose on the forehead. He was clammy but his vitals were stable. The doctors had just left, telling Gabriela and Angel he was the same and they'd check back in another hour.

Carefully, she withdrew her arm from under the seven-year-old and slid off the hospital bed. Gabriela, halfheartedly clicking through Facebook, glanced up. "Can I get you something?"

Her friend's worried face comforted the mother to a small degree. To know she wasn't alone helped keep her from breaking down into a worthless puddle. She thought Duke was still probably around, too, but he hadn't been in the room in a while.

"I'm going to go find the doctor. I'll be back before the doctors make their next rounds. I trust you to watch over him, Gabriela. Call me if something happens." She left before Gabriela could argue further. She had to do this.

On her way out, Angel locked eyes with the head of pediatrics, who stood behind the desk, on her phone.

The doctor hung up and approached. "Listen, I was right. I went back and I found the file of two kids who've died from asthma this year. Both files mentioned asthma inhalers with no markings. But no one thought to test the contents. I just tested Jose's—there is no medicine. It's a placebo." She stuck her hands in the pocket of her lab coat. "All three were given to the parents by the same doctor."

"Dr. Collins," said Angel.

She nodded. Her face was heavy with sadness. "I don't

know how a doctor could do this—how anyone could, for that matter." She put her hand on Angel's shoulder. "But I've been talking to the police lieutenant. If you're willing to wear a wire and confront this man, get him to talk, a detective is on his way to the clinic right now. He'll meet you there."

"Of course I am. If what you say is true, he's the reason my baby is suffering." Angel started to go, but then turned back. "I'm gonna make this quick. Take care of my baby."

Angel's stride lengthened with each step down the long hallway, fueled by a rage burning hotter and hotter. She barely remembered the walk out of the hospital and the few blocks to the clinic, fueled by hate. By the time Angel reached the clinic doors, she was the sun, bordering on supernova.

A man in a suit jacket and khakis had been leaning against the building but stood up when she approached. "You Angel Gomez?"

"Yes."

"The peds doctor from University called the precinct and told me what's going on. You think you can get him on tape?"

"I'm going to at least try."

The nondescript man handed her a silver cylinder the size of a short pencil. "Just press the top button. It's a recorder, but it's also a two-way radio. I'll be able to hear everything you say, and I'm gonna be right outside the door."

She trembled as she approached the doctor's office. It was late. He might have left, this could be for nothing. The charge nurse hadn't seen him go, though. She adjusted the microphone—which she'd slid into her panties. It was now or never. She opened the door without knocking. "Dr. Collins!"

The doctor was in. He dropped his pen and sat up straight behind the desk, his black hair falling over his high forehead, his eyes big Os. "Angel?" he squeaked, then cleared his throat. "I'm surprised to see you."

"I've changed my mind." She closed the door to the office. *That detective better live up to his word. If he doesn't get in here in time, I'll be arrested for a brutal murder.* "I need to finish this. I have to get my nursing degree. Tell me what to do and I'll do it."

He slit his eyes, suspicious. "What are you talking about?"

"I'm not joking around. What, you think I'm wearing a wire? Here." She slid off her top, trying to be slinky, revealing the same bra as that morning. "My son is sick. The only way I can help him is if I'm working a decent job." She kicked off her shoes. Untying the bottoms of her scrubs, she asked him, "So, what can I do? How do you want me?"

He stayed seated, watching her.

She wriggled a hand partway down the waistband of her pants and massaged her lower stomach. He licked his lips. She ran her hands up over her breasts, and then, as her hands slid back down over her skin, she pulled the bra down, channeling what she'd learned from every B-grade stripper movie she'd ever seen. She let the material drop back into place as her hands continued south. She let her hand go all the way below her waistband, her eyes drooping, her head tilting back. "Mmm."

"Come here." The doctor finally spoke, his voice guttural.

"Oh, you like that? Ohh."

He stood up, quickly moving toward her. "Hot little Latina bitch. Take those pants off, whore."

She let him get just in front of her, putting one palm out. "Will you sign my evaluation if I just let you watch? I can make it worth your while."

"You want me to sign, darlin'? You're gonna ride me."

She gulped. *Stay calm.* "Yeah? Then I want some more asthma medicine."

He laughed and tugged on the drawstring of her pants, as if he was flirting with her. "You get me off and you can have the whole drawer." He ran a finger up her stomach. "It's not like I pay for that crap."

She snapped her head forward and yanked her hand out of her pants, yelling into the cylinder, "Did you hear that?"

Dr. Collins's hand shot out and locked onto her wrist, layered over the bruises he'd created that morning. She dropped the recorder.

"What is that? Is that a mic?"

"Yes, asshole!" She cocked her knee back, aimed, and brought up her leg with the force of a woman brimful of storming fury.

By the time the detective could get the door open, Dr. Collins was on the ground, crying for mercy. The detective cocked an eyebrow at her.

She shrugged. "He was attacking me. I had to defend myself."

As the detective helped the weeping man to his feet and retrieved the recording device, Angel went to Dr. Collins's desk, picked up her stack of evaluations, and was about to walk out the door when the detective stopped her. She caught her breath, afraid he was going to make her hand over the papers. Instead, he insisted she stop at the police precinct and sign an affidavit.

"We gotta make sure this piece of shit stays put, am I right?" he asked, holding the broken man in a firm grip.

"But—"

Her cell rang. It was Gabriela. "What is it? Is he okay?" she shouted into the phone, watching carefully as the detective put handcuffs on the pale wrists of her ex-boss.

"Honey, honey, calm down," said an excited Gabriela. "He's woken up. He's groggy, but he's okay. The doc says he's got all his cogs in place."

"His cognitive abilities are intact?"

"Sure. He ain't stupid, is what she's sayin'. Where are you, anyway? What is that yowling?"

It was Dr. Collins, crying as his Miranda rights were read to him.

"Listen, I have one small thing I have to do. Can you hold down the fort for a while longer? Give Jose a big kiss for me? Tell him I'll be there as soon as I can."

"I don't under—"

"It's important. You'll see." She hung up and turned back to the cop. "Okay. Can I get a ride to the station?" She grinned at Collins, so cute in his handcuffs. "But I'll let you sit in the caged backseat by yourself. Best you get used to that now."

Chapter Twenty-four

Maybe I should give Duke a chance. The image of him running across the field with Jose, saving her little boy's life, melted her heart. How could it not? And his heroism came on the heels of him admitting he'd walked away from the Bronx Bolts rather than take pain pills and performance enhancing drugs. What was there not to like? There was no ugliness in him, not like she'd believed. *And he's made me feel that what I found ugly about myself could be lovable . . . He's made me believe I could be part of his world.*

"Angel?"

She was standing in the middle of the precinct, not expecting to hear her name, and certainly not from such a melodic voice. Yet there he was, Duke, propping himself up on crutches but perfect nonetheless, even with half his face hidden under a baseball cap.

Oh. Crutches. His long sprint with Jose took on a whole new meaning.

Before she could dwell on it too long, he said, "Are you okay?" He was anxious, confused. "Why aren't you with Jose?"

"I'm fine. And Jose's actually fine—he woke up! What are you doing here? I thought you were at the hospital . . ."

Then, behind him, she saw Regina. The anorexic model was being escorted by two burly policemen; she was fighting against the silver bracelets they'd placed on her. She was taken down a back hall, kicking and spitting.

"*Que diablos?!*" Angel said, her jaw dropping to her chest.

Before Duke could answer, Dr. Collins was escorted through the room, wearing bracelets that were an exact match to Regina's.

A sudden glee sprang up in her chest. *Oh, that copycat,* she thought, a childish giggle bursting free. She laughed even harder when Duke followed her line of sight and realized she was staring at Dr. Collins. The pitcher did a double take, and then a triple take.

The doctor spotted Duke at the same time. He jounced his long, weak frame, trying to shake himself free. "Look here, you gentlemen have clearly made a mistake!" he shouted to a detective, who didn't seem to hear him. "It's *that* man you want, the young black man over there. He's been taking drugs."

"I—I—What . . ." Duke, wide-eyed, swung around to face her.

Angel put her fingertips on his arm. "I think we have a lot to talk about."

The police officer pushing Collins across the bullpen glanced over at Duke and then took a second glance, smiling wide. "Hey! Aren't you the Duke? Can you sign an autograph for me?"

Half an hour later, Angel helped Duke out of a cab in front of the hospital. They'd both forgotten about the press. A few die-hard journalists loitered by the lobby doors and were happily surprised to see Duke returning, though they'd had no idea he'd even left.

"I'm not going to hide anymore," Duke told her, trying to get the crutches under him. "Not going to hide what's happening, or who I'm with."

"They know who you're with. Supposedly." She shut the cab door and stepped close, helping him. "That was the whole point of you hanging out with me, remember? To give reporters a story your boss could believe?"

"You're not still mad, are you?"

"No. You know what? I'm not mad at all."

"Well, we don't want to deprive these guys of their shot at the big time, do we? Maybe we should give them another photo op?" His big, green puppy eyes became shy. "For real this time?"

"You mean you want *me* to give *you* another shot." She

took off his baseball cap and threw it to a photographer. "Lucky for you, I'd already decided that."

This time, when they kissed in front of the cameras, it lasted for a long time.

Epilogue

One year later

"Go, Jose! Run!" shouted Angel.

"Girl, you goin' to hurt yourself. You let Auntie cheer for both of us. Er, for the three of us." Gabriela smiled, patting Angel's pregnant belly before screaming at the top of her lungs for the eight-year-old running the bases. They both cheered when Jose slid home. But it was Duke who really made a spectacle of himself, hoisting the grinning kid onto his shoulders, jogging with him back to the dugout like Jose had just won them the World Series.

Well, my baby did just make his first home run. Angel smiled. Who better to celebrate with him than the Duke—his new coach, who had new pins in his ankle and a year of physical therapy under his belt. And, of course, he was also Jose's new daddy. Her son and the retired pitcher were two peas in a pod, and Angel couldn't be happier. Duke came to as close to perfect as a man can get.

"Aren't you going to be late for work? You need a ride?"

"No. The company is sending a car."

"Well, lah-dee-dah."

"The company" was a new nonprofit research center for childhood asthma, under the umbrella of the National Pediatric Association. Duke was the center's spokesperson, with Jose and Willis at his side most of the time. It was a family affair—Angel was a nurse at the research center's medical complex. The name on the building was The Kinley Smith Asthma Clinic.

Angel rubbed her belly with satisfaction, breathed deeply to take in the smell of cut grass and damp earth, and reveled in the perfect moment.

About the Authors

Ziv Sade

EVELYN LOZADA is a high-profile American-Latina reality television personality, entrepreneur, author, and philanthropist. She is best known for her role on VH1's hit series *Basketball Wives* (2010–present), OWN's hit series *Livin' Lozada* (2015), as the author of *Inner Circle*, the first installment of the book series The Wives Association (2012), and as the creator of "Healthy Boricua," a Puerto Rican lifestyle guide to healthy living. She has become a national trendsetter, a "go-to" fitness expert, a jewelry designer, a fashion and beauty maven, social media royalty, and a stimulating voice and proactive supporter of causes that affect women and girls through the Evelyn Lozada Foundation. Evelyn is a Bronx native, and a mother of two, Shaniece Hairston and Carl Leo Crawford, who currently resides in Los Angeles.

Grauwen Photography

HOLLY LÖRINCZ is a successful collaborative writer and owner of Lörincz Literary Services. She is an award-winning novelist of *Smart Mouth* and *The Everything Girl* and co-author of the bestselling novels *Crown Heights* and *How to Survive a Day in Prison*. Holly currently lives in Oregon.